SB

Poems

Sorrow's Kitchen
My Tongue in Other Cheeks: Selected Translations

As editor

Ash of Stars: On the Writing of Samuel R. Delany
Jazz Guitars
The Guitar in Jazz

Other

The Guitar Players
Difficult Lives
Saint Glinglin by Raymond Queneau (translator)
Gently into the Land of the Meateaters
Chester Himes: A Life
A James Sallis Reader

SALT RIVER

A Novel

JAMES SALLIS

NO EXIT PRESS

First published in the UK in 2008 by No Exit Press,
P.O.Box 394, Harpenden, Herts, AL5 1XJ
www.noexit.co.uk

A CIP catalogue record for this book is available
from the British Library.

ISBN 978-1- 84243-277-8

2 4 6 8 10 9 7 5 3 1

Typeset by Ellipsis Books Limited, Glasgow

Printed and bound in Great Britain by
J.H.Haynes & Co Ltd, Yeovil, Somerset

*To Odie Piker
and Ant Bee—
for putting on The Dog*

CHAPTER ONE

SOMETIMES YOU JUST HAVE to see how much music you can make with what you have left. Val told me that, seconds before I heard the crash of her wineglass against the porch floor, looked up, and only then became aware of the shot that preceded it, two years ago now.

The town doesn't have much left. I've watched it wither away until some days you'd think the first strong wind could take it. I'm not sure how much I have left either. With the town, it's all economics. As for me, I think maybe I've seen a few too many people die, witnessed too much unbearable sadness that still had somehow to be borne. I remember Tracy Caulding up in Memphis telling me about a science fiction story where these immortals would every century or so swim across a pool that relieved them of their memories, then they could go on. I wanted a swim in that pool.

Doc Oldham and I were sitting on the bench outside Manny's Dollar $tore. Doc had stopped by to show off his new dance step and, worn out from the thirty-second performance, had staggered outside to rest up a spell, so I was resting up with him.

'Used to be Democrats in these parts,' Doc said. 'Strange creatures, but they bred well. 'Bout any direction you looked, that's all you'd see.'

Doc had retired, and his place had been taken by a new doctor, Bill Wilford, who looked all of nineteen years old. Doc now spent most of his time sitting outside. He spent a lot of it, too, saying things like that.

'Where'd they all get to, Turner?' He looked at me, pulling his head back, turtlelike, to focus. I had to wonder what portion of the world outside actually made it through those cataracts, how much of it got caught up in there forever. 'Town's dried up, same as a riverbed. What the hell you stayin' here for?'

He grabbed at a knee to stop the twitching from the exercise minutes ago. His hands looked like faded pink rubber gloves. All the pigment got burned out a long time back, he said, when he was a chemist, before medical school.

'Yeah, I know,' he went on, 'what the hell are any of us staying here for? Granted, the town wasn't much to start with. Never was meant to be. Just grew up here, like a weed. Farms all about, back then. People start thinking about going to town of a weekend, pick up flour and the like, there has to *be* a town. So they made one. Drew straws, for all I know. See who had to move into the damn thing.'

A thumb-size grasshopper came kiting across the street and landed on Doc's sleeve. The two of them regarded one another.

'Youngsters used to be all around, too, like them Democrats. Nowadays the ones that don't just get *born* old and stay that way, they up and leave soon's they can.' Looking down, he told the grasshopper: 'You should, too.'

Doc liked people but was never much for social amenities, one of those who came and went as he pleased and said pretty much what he thought. Now that he didn't have anything to do, sometimes you got the feeling that the second cup of coffee you'd offered might stretch to meet your newborn's graduation. He knew it, too, duly noting and relishing every sign of unease, every darting eye, every shuffled foot. 'Wonder is, I'm here at all,' he'd tell you. 'My own goddamn miracle of medical science. Got more wrong with me than a hospital full of leftovers. Asthma, diabetes, heart trouble. Enough metal in me to sink a good-size fishing boat.'

'What you are,' I'd tell him, 'is a miracle of stubbornness.'

'Just hugging the good earth, Turner. Just hugging the good earth.'

The grasshopper stepped down to his knee, sat there a moment, then took off, with a thrill of wings, back out over the street.

'Least *somebody* listens,' Doc said. 'Back when I was an intern . . .'

Apparently a page had been turned in the chronicle playing inside his head. I waited for his coughing fit to subside.

'Back when I was an intern – it was like high school machine shop, those days. Learn to use the hacksaw, pliers, clamps, the whatsits. More like *Jeopardy* now – how much obscure stuff can you remember? Anyway, I was working with all these kids, all in a ward together. A lot of cystic fibrosis – not that we knew what it was. Kids who'd got the butt end of everything.

'There was this one, ugliest little thing you ever saw, body all used up, with this barrel chest, skin like leather, fingers like baseball bats. But she had this pretty name, Leilani. Made you think of flowers and perfume and music. An attending told us one day that the truth was, Leilani didn't exist anymore, hadn't really been alive for years, it was just the infection, the pseudomonas in her, that went on living – moving her body around, breathing, responding.'

He looked off in the direction the grasshopper had taken.

'That's how I feel some days.'

'Doc, I just want you to know, any time you feel like dropping by to cheer me up, don't hesitate.'

'Never have. Spread it around.'

'You do that, all right.'

He waited a moment before asking, 'And how are *you* doing?'

'I'm here.'

'That's what it comes down to, Turner. That's what it comes down to.'

'One might hope for more.'

'One does. Always. So one gets off one's beloved butt and goes looking. Then, next thing you know, the sticks you used to knock fruit out of a tree have got sharpened up to spears and the spears have turned to guns, and there you are: countries, politicians, TV, designer clothes. Descartes said all our ills come from a man being unable to sit alone, quietly, in a room.'

'I did that a lot.'

'Ain't sure a prison cell counts.'

'Before. And after. The ills found me anyway.'

'Yeah. They'll do that, won't they? Like a dog that gets the taste for blood. Can't break him of it.'

Odie Piker drove by in his truck, cylinders banging. Thing had started out life as a Dodge. Over the years so many parts had been replaced – galvanized steel welded on as fenders, rust spots filled and painted over in whatever color came to hand, four or five rebuilt clutches and a motor or two dropped in – that there was probably nothing left of the original. Nor, I think, had it at any time in all those years ever been washed or cleaned out. Dust from the fallout of bombs tested in the fifties lurked in its seams, and back under the seat you'd find wrappers for food products long since extinct.

Doors eased shut on pneumatics as Donna and Sally Ann left City Hall for lunch at Jay's Diner. Minutes later, Mayor Sims stepped out the side door and stood brushing at his sport coat. When he saw us, his hand shifted into a sketchy wave.

'Frangible,' Doc proclaimed, his mind on yet another track.

'Okay.'

'Frangible. What we all are – what life is. Fragile. Easily broken. Mean the same. But neither gets it near the way *frangible* does.'

He looked off at the mayor, who had gotten in his car and was just sitting there.

'Two schools of thought. One has it we're best off using simple words, plain words. That fancier ones only serve to obscure meaning – wrap it in swaddling clothes. Other side says that takes everything down to the lowest common denominator, that thought is complex and if you want to get close to what's really meant you have to choose words carefully, words that catch up gradations, nuances . . . You know this shit, Turner.'

'A version of it.'

'Versions are what we have. Of truth, our histories, ourselves. Hell, you know that, too.'

I smiled.

'Frangible Henry over there's trying to talk himself out of going to see his lady friend up by Elaine.' He gave the town's name a hard accent. *E*laine. 'But it's Thursday. And whichever side of the argument you pick to look at it from, he'll lose.'

'You never cease to amaze me, Doc.'

'I'm common as horseflies, Turner. We all are, however much we go on making out that it's otherwise . . . Guess we should both be about our work. If we had some, that is. Anything you need to be doing?'

'Always paperwork.'

'Accounts for eighty percent of the workforce, people just moving papers from one place to another. Though nowadays I guess there ain't much actual paper involved. Half the *rest* of the workforce spends its time trying to find papers that got put in the wrong place. Well,' he said, 'there goes Henry off to Elaine.'

We sat watching as the mayor's butt-sprung old Buick waddled down the street. A huge crow paced it, sweeping figure eights above, then darted away. Thought it was some lumbering beast about to drop in its tracks, maybe.

Doc pushed to his feet and stood rocking. 'They

say when you stare into the abyss, the abyss stares back. I think they're wrong, Turner. I think it only winks.'

With that sage remark Doc left, to be about his business and leave me to mine, as he put it, and once he was gone I sat there alone still resting up, wondering what my business might be.

Alone was exactly what I'd thought my business was when I came here. Now I found myself at the center of this tired old town, part of a community, even of a family of sorts. Never had considered myself much of a talker either. But with Val conversation had just gone on and on, past weary late afternoons into bleary early mornings, and I was forever remembering things she'd said to me.

Sometimes you just have to see how much music you can make with what you have left.

Or the time we were talking about my prison years and the years after, as a therapist, and she told me: 'You're a matchbook, Turner. You keep on setting fire to yourself. But somehow at the same time you always manage to kindle fires in others.'

Did I?

All I knew for certain was that for too much of my life people around me wound up dying. I wanted that to stop. I wanted a lot of things to stop.

The car Billy Bates was in, for instance. I wanted it to stop – can't begin to tell you how very much I wish it had stopped – when it came plowing headlong down the street in front of me, before it crashed through the front wall of City Hall.

CHAPTER TWO

A WONDER, always, to watch Doc work. You'd swear he was giving things no more attention than tying a shoelace, but he was well and surely *in there*, and nothing got by him. By the time I'd crossed the street he had Billy out of the car, one hand clutching the back of his shirt, the other cradling his head. Man can barely stand, and here he is hauling someone out of a car. Had Billy on the sidewalk in no time flat, feeling for pulses, prodding and poking.

Donna and Sally Ann came out of the diner, Donna with half a BLT in her hand. Three steps past the door, a slice of pickle fell out and she looked down at it, vacantly, the way others stood staring at the hole in the wall plugged by Billy's Buick Regal. Country music, or what passes for country music these days, played on the radio. Someone reached into the car and turned it off.

'Pupils look okay,' Doc said. 'Not blown, anyway. You want to go on back in the office there and bring me out some tape, Turner? Any kind should do her, long as it's heavy. Duct tape be perfect. I assume,' he said at the same volume, but to the gathering crowd, 'that one of you has had sense enough to call Rory?'

'Mabel's tracking him down,' Sally Ann told him. Mabel, who'd been at it long enough to have been (some said) ordained by Alexander Graham Bell himself, was our local telephone operator, unofficial historian, and town crier. 'She's also trying to find Milly.'

As I came out, Doc pulled a loose-leaf binder from the backseat of the car and slid it under Billy's head and shoulders. He tore off a length of tape and turned the ends in, so that it stuck to itself, to make a cradle for Billy's head. Then he started taping, back and forth, around and down, till head and notebook were a piece. That done, he splinted the left wrist, where a bone protruded, with tape and a paperback book also from the car. He sat with his legs straight out in front of him, picking glass out of Billy's face with finger and thumb, wiping them on his pants.

Everyone wanted to know where the mayor was, but Doc never batted an eye.

'Damn,' he said afterward, as we waited, 'that felt

gooood,' dropping a couple extra *o*'s in there. 'I'm of half a mind to kick that boy doctor out and take back my office.' After a moment he added, 'He's good, though. I made sure of that.'

'You miss it, don't you?'

'Hell, Turner, my age, I miss damn near everything.'

Heads turned as Rory's ambulance came up the middle of Main Street. Once a delivery van for the local builders' supply, the old Pontiac now doubled as hearse, and letters from the store's name still showed beneath new paint when light fell just right. Rory had taken time to pull back the curtains inside. He got out, wearing hip boots and the smell of the river, leaving the door open. Lonnie climbed out the other side, in knee boots, and stood looking down at his younger son without saying anything.

Doc's wrappings made it look as though a mummy's head had taken over Billy's body. Of course, in Lonnie's view something had taken over Billy long ago.

I remembered when I first met Billy, how I thought he might be the closest thing to an innocent human being I'd ever known. He was dressed all in black back then, with multiple piercings and no discernible sense of direction any of us could make out, parents included, just a sweet kid kind of happily adrift. He'd dropped out of school not long after, not dropped out so much as just, well, drifted out. Missed a few days, then a week, and never went back. Worked at the hardware store a while, but that didn't last either. Then he was playing drums with a band that worked a lot outside town in the bars along Old Highway, but for some reason, the way he looked, his quietness, he was a magnet for trouble. People kept stepping up to him and he wouldn't back down. Don Lee and I'd answered our share of call-outs only to find Billy at the other end. Bar brawls, traffic incidents, domestic disturbances. Then, a year ago, he'd got married, gone back to the hardware store, and things were looking good for him. Few months later, he disappeared. We found his truck out on the Hill Road By-pass where he'd pulled it over and flagged down the bus headed toward Little Rock. Milly, his wife, said she'd often go looking for him and find him sitting in the basement sawing wood up into smaller and smaller pieces.

I helped Rory load Billy into the ambulance, then went over and stood by Lonnie.

Two guys off fishing, looking forward to a quiet, easy day. Sandwiches, maybe a beer or two, bait bucket standing by, drowsy sun in the sky. Now this. *Frangible*, like Doc said. How brittle our lives are, how tentative, every day of them, every moment.

Once I'd been up at the camp while Isaiah Stillman was, as he put it, 'doing laundry' – balancing the books on the family funds he managed. That evening he was cleaning out old folders and files, had them all lined up in the recycle bin. 'We're never more than a keystroke away from oblivion, you know,' he said, and hit the key to delete the contents.

So one minute Lonnie's off fishing, the next he's standing on Main Street looking down at his bloody, broken son.

Or you're together on the porch then suddenly she's gone and you have to start finding out how much music you can make with what you have left.

'You're not going to tell me everything's going to be okay, are you, Turner.'

I shook my head.

'Or start with "If there's anything I can do," then trail off.'

'No.'

'Course you're not.'

Lonnie stepped over to the Regal and shut the door. One of Billy's shoes was just outside it.

'You ever read a story called "Thus I Refute Beelzy"?' Lonnie asked.

I said I hadn't.

'About a boy whose father forces him to admit that his imaginary friend isn't real. Kid holds out a long time, but he finally gives in. At the end of the story, all they find of the old man on the stairs is a shoe with the foot still in it.'

He walked around to the car's rear. 'That the right license plate, you think?'

'I'll run it.' The nuts had the same grime as the plate itself. No signs of abrasion around them. 'Doesn't look to have been changed, though.'

'First thing we have to find out is whose car this is.'

'Absolutely. I'll get right on it. Oh, and . . .'

'Yeah?'

'Good to have you back, Sheriff.'

CHAPTER THREE

THIS TIME IT WAS the sound of a motorcycle, not a Jeep. It came up around the lake in late sunlight, echo racketing off the water and the cabin wall behind me as I stood thinking about Lonnie, that first time. I'd been here a few months then. The sheriff had come to pay a visit, and to ask me to help with a murder.

The banjo case was slung on the bike behind him, neck sticking up so that, at the distance, for a moment there seemed to be a second head peering over his shoulder. He dismounted, stood, and nodded. He'd gone wiry, body and hair alike, but his grin hadn't changed at all.

'Things about the same, I see. Still a nice quiet place to live.'

'That *was* you in town, then.' He'd been standing off from the rest, in the closest thing we had to an alley, a space by the boarded-up feed store that caught runoff from adjacent roofs and where, following each rain, crops of mushrooms sprang up.

'You didn't say anything.'

'I figure a man doesn't declare himself, he has reasons.'

Eldon followed me onto the porch. I hadn't sat out on it much since that day, but the chairs I'd strung together with twine were still in place.

'What *was* all that commotion?' he said, settling into one and tucking the banjo case between his feet.

I told him about Billy.

'Lonnie's boy, right?'

I nodded.

'He gonna be okay?'

'We'll know more tomorrow.'

Eldon peered off into the trees. A mild wind was starting up, the way it does most nights. 'It really is peaceful here. I forget.'

'Long as you don't look too closely.'

'Right. What was it someone said, Peace is only the time it takes to reload? . . . I wasn't sure I wanted to come out here, you know.'

'But you did.'

'Looks like.'

'And you rode in on a horse. Where's the wagon?'

'Val's Volvo? Sucker down in Texas took it out.

Coming out of a rest stop, never looked. Had to be going eighty or better by the time he hit the highway. And by the time I saw him it was too late, I was bouncing back and forth between a semi and the guardrail doing my best not to crash into someone else. You'll be glad to know the Volvo's rep holds up. Safest car around. There it is, pretty much demolished, but Homer and I don't have a scratch.'

'Homer?'

'Val told me she sometimes thought of the Whyte Laydie as Homer.'

'Blind poet?'

He shrugged. 'You get my letters?'

'Got them. And would have answered them, if I'd had any kind of address.' In the months following Val's death, those letters, telling me where Eldon had been, where he was headed next, rambling on about what he was thinking and the people he'd met, had become important to me. 'When they stopped, I had to figure either they'd served whatever purpose you had in writing them, or that the purpose didn't matter anymore.'

'Everything have to have a purpose?'

'Purpose, reason, motivation. Pick your word. Not that we ever actually understand our motives – but we seldom act arbitrarily.'

'Sounds suspiciously like you believe it all has a meaning.'

'Not the way we think, locked as we are into cause and effect. Some grand design? No. But patterns are everywhere.'

'Maybe it's all just messages in a bottle.'

'As you recall, I spent a few years of my life decoding those. Messages in a bottle generally come in two flavors. SAVE ME! Or FUCK YOU ALL.'

He glanced back at me before the trees regained his interest. Fault lines at eyes and mouth, hair chopped almost to his scalp and going a stately gray. Two years. And he looked to have aged ten.

'Don't know as I'd ever written a letter before. I can remember at the time thinking: Man plays a hundred-year-old banjo, he might do well to put his hand to a letter now and again, seems only right. Which sounds like something *she*'d say, doesn't it?'

'She's in us all, Eldon. Part of who we are, the way we see the world.'

'You ever think maybe people should be allowed to just pass on, that we shouldn't have to carry them around inside us forever?'

'Of course. But we do, right alongside what we've done with our own lives.'

'Or haven't. Yeah.'

None of us, Lonnie, Don Lee, J. T., Eldon, or myself, had ever openly spoken of what happened up in Memphis the day after Val's death. Each had been out of pocket then: Don Lee under the weather, Lonnie returning from a business trip, J. T. checking in back home in Seattle, Eldon absent from his gig.

'So I'd be sitting there, in Bumfuck, Texas, or Grasslimb, Iowa, writing on motel stationery when some was to be had, on tablets from the 7-Eleven when it wasn't, and I'd be remembering how you told me that so much of what you'd been taught about counseling – that it's imperative to talk things out, drag feelings into daylight – how so much of that was dead wrong.'

'Humankind has a purblind passion to find some single idea that will explain *everything*. Religion, alien visitation, Marxism, string theory. Psychology.'

'And I'd remember your saying that people don't change.'

'What I said was, we adapt. Everything that was there before is still there, always will be. The trick's in how we come to terms with it.'

'I'd think about all that, and I'd go on writing. Then one day I stopped. For no particular reason – same as I'd started.'

Dark was coming on. Out in the near border of trees a pair of eyes, a hawk's or owl's, caught light. From deep in the woods came a bobcat's scream.

'*I*'ve changed,' Eldon said.

I waited and, when nothing else was forthcoming, went in and poured half a jelly glass of the homemade mash Nathan brought 'round on a regular basis.

Designer, he'd taken to calling it, having picked up the modish epithet somewhere. God only knows where that might have been, since he never left the woods, had no radio, hadn't set eyes on a newspaper since around V-day, and met with a shotgun anyone who set foot on his land. But he loved the word and used it every chance he got, grinning through teeth like cypress stumps.

By the time I came back out, that quickly, dark had claimed everything at ground level; only a narrow band of light above the trees remained. Eldon was sitting with his head on the back of the chair, eyes closed. He spoke without opening them.

'When I was twelve – I remember, because I'd just started playing guitar, after giving up on school band and a cheap trumpet that kept falling apart on me. Anyway, I was twelve, sitting out on the porch practicing, it was one of those Silvertones with the amp in the case, only the amp didn't work so I'd bought it for next to nothing, and this mockingbird staggers up to me. Can't fly, and looks better than half dead already. Dehydrated, weak, wasted. It's like he's chosen me, I'm his last chance.

'I got a dish of water for him, some dry cat food, lashed sticks together with twine to make a cage. Too many dogs and cats around to leave him out.

'Whatever was wrong – broken wing, most likely – he never got over it. Spent the last eight months of his life on that back porch looking out at a world he was no longer part of.'

Eldon reached over and snagged the glass from me, took a long swallow. I remembered our sitting together in The Shack out on State Road 41 after someone had smashed his guitar and tried to start a fight, remembered his telling me that night why he never drank.

'I'm sitting there trying to keep a bird alive, and all around me people are dying and there's two or three wars going on. What kind of sense does that make?'

He handed the glass back.

'They think I killed someone, John.'

'Did you?'

'I don't know.'

We sat watching the moon coast through high branches.

'Been a hell of a ride,' he said after a while, 'this life.'

'Always. If you just pay attention.'

CHAPTER FOUR

LONNIE WAS SETTING a coffee mug down by June's computer when I walked in. She handed me a call slip. Since when did we have call slips? The name Sgt Haskell, with a tiny smiley face for the period in *Sgt*, and a number in Hazelwood, which was a couple of counties over, tucked into the state's upper corner like hair into an armpit. I looked at Lonnie. He couldn't have taken this?

He ambled over with a mug for me. Fresh pot, from the smell of it. 'The sergeant would only talk to the sheriff, thank you very much.'

And that was me, since I'd failed to step backward fast enough. I'd stepped back sure enough, resolutely refusing the job again and again, but when I stepped back that last time and looked around, there was no one else left. Lonnie had retired. After a little over a year in the catbird seat, my daughter J. T. had found she missed the barely restrained chaos (though that was not the way she put it) and headed back to Seattle. Don Lee stayed on as deputy, but he was a little like Eldon's mockingbird, he'd never quite got over what happened to him.

Haskell answered on the second ring and said he'd call right back. I could have been anyone, naturally, but I had a feeling this had less to do with precaution or procedure than it did with things being kinda slow over in Hazelwood.

'You had a vehicle up on LETS,' he said once we'd exchanged pleasantries concerning families (I had none, he had six maiden aunts), weather ('not so bad of a morning'), and a fishing update. 'Buick Regal, '81.' He read off the VIN. 'MVA?'

'Right.'

'Nothing too bad, I hope.'

'We'll know more soon.'

'Sorry to hear that. If this is any help, the car's from over our way. Belonged to Miss Augusta Chorley, but seeing as the lady is pushing eighty, from the *far* side, some say, the vehicle's been out of circulation awhile.'

'Chances are good it's going to be out of circulation permanently now.' Now that it had taken out half of City Hall. I told him what had happened. 'We'll have to hold it for a few days, naturally, but please let

Miss Chorley know that we'll get it back to her as soon as possible. And if you can give me the NIC number and fax a copy of the report—'

'Would have done that already if I'd had one. Car wasn't stolen, Sheriff.'

I waited. Sergeant Haskell there in his cubbyhole of an office next to Liberty Bank over in Hazelwood, me looking out at Main Street through spaces between sheets of plywood Eddie Wilson had nailed in place: two cool, experienced law enforcement officials going about our daily business.

'Driver a young man, early twenties? Slight build, dark hair, flannel-shirt-and-jeans type?'

'That's him. Billy Bates.'

'One of yours?'

'Grew up here. Been gone awhile.'

'I see.' Over there in Hazelwood, Sergeant Haskell cleared his throat. I tried the coffee. 'Boy'd been doing some work for old Miss Chorley is what I'm hearing. Lady lives in this house, all that's left of what used to be the biggest plantation hereabouts, down to two barely usable rooms now, nothing but scrub and dead soil all around. House itself's been going to ground for fifty or sixty years now. No family that anyone knows of. Old lady's all alone out there, wouldn't answer the door if someone *did* show up, but no one does. Your boy – Billy, right?'

'Right.'

'He'd moved into an old hunter's shack out by the lake here. Started fixing it up, making a good job of it, some say. Kind of living on air, though. Picked up part-time work delivering groceries for Carl Sanderson, which has to be how he met Miss Chorley. Next thing anyone knows, the porch is back up where it's supposed to be, house has old wood coming off, new paint going on.'

'And the car?'

'Rumor is that no one in the family ever had much use for banks and the old lady has a fortune out there. Under the floorboards, buried out by the willow tree in a false grave – you know how people talk. If money ever changed hands, it never showed. Boy had one pair of pants and a couple of mismatched socks to his name. But Miss Chorley up and gave him the car. Maybe as payment, maybe because she had no use for it. Maybe just because she liked him. Had to be some lonely, all by herself out there all these years.'

'And you know this how?'

'Week or so back, Seth's out by the old mining road making his usual rounds and recognizes the Buick, pulls it over. Boy had the title right there, signed over to him by the old lady.'

'Doesn't sound as though he'd done enough work to earn it. Jacked up the porch, patched some walls—'

'I don't think he was done here. Stopped by the

grocery store, on the way out of town from the look of it, to tell Carl Sanderson he'd be away a few days, back early in the week.'

'Thanks, Sergeant.'

'No problem. Anything else, you let me know. Hope things turn out for the boy.'

'We all do.'

While I was talking to Sergeant Haskell, a man had come into the office, standing just inside the door staring at the plywood sheets Eddie had nailed up. Fiftyish, wearing a powder blue sport coat over maroon slacks with a permanent crease gone a few shades lighter than the rest. A mustache ran out in two wings from his nostrils, as though he had sneezed it into being.

He'd been talking to Lonnie. Now, as I hung up, Lonnie pointed a finger in my direction and the man started over. Most of the hair on top was gone. Most of the sole was gone on the outside of his shoes, too. Not a heavy man, yet he had the appearance of one.

'Sheriff Turner? Jed Baxter.'

June brought a chair over, and he sat, putting him a head or so below my eye level. Just as he gave the appearance of being a heavy man, he had also seemed on first impression taller. Attitude.

'What can I do for you?'

He was going for the wallet and badge, but I waved

it off as obvious. He nodded. 'PD in Fort Worth, Texas.'

'Then you're a long way from home.'

'Tell the truth, things up this way don't look a hell of a lot different from back home. Just smaller.'

'Again: What can I do for you?'

'Right. You know an Eldon Brown, I believe.' When I said nothing, he continued. 'He went missing on us. And we have some questions for him. Man hasn't left much of a footprint in his life. We started looking into it, this is one of the places that came up.'

'He lived here a while. As Lonnie no doubt told you.'

'That he did. Gone, what, two years now?'

'About that.'

'No contact since then?'

'Handful of letters, at first. Then those stopped.'

'Something happen that caused him to leave?'

He smiled, eyes never leaving mine. Like many cops, Baxter had rudimentary interviewing skills, equal parts bluster, attempted ingratiation, and silence. Eldon used to talk about bass players he'd worked with, guys who had two patterns they just moved up or down the neck. It was like that. I smiled back, waited, and said 'Nothing.'

'Don't suppose you'd have any idea where he was heading when he left.'

Texas, I said, and told him about the festivals.

'Musician. Yeah, that's most of what we do know.'

Again the smile. Hair that had migrated from the mother country of skull had colonized the ears, from which it sprouted like sheaves of wheat. I sat imagining them waving gently in the current from the revolving fan across the room.

'Who would he be likely to contact, if he was back?'

'It's a small town, Detective. Everyone here knows everyone else.'

Baxter took his time peering about the room, then at Lonnie and June, who obviously had been listening. June looked down. Lonnie didn't.

'You don't say a lot, do you, Sheriff? Odd, that you haven't even asked why I'm looking for Brown.'

'Not really.'

His eyebrows lifted.

'You may have reason for not telling me. And if you *are* going to tell me, you will, in your own time. Meanwhile, I can't help but notice there's been no mention of a CAPIS warrant.'

Baxter made a sound, kind of the bastard offspring of *harrumph* and a snort. 'I see . . . That how you live 'round here?'

'We try, some of us.'

'Well, then.' He stood, tugging at his maroon slacks. The lighter-shaded crease jumped like a guide wire, seemingly independent of the rest. 'Thank you for your time, Sheriff.'

With a nod to the others, he left. Through the window we watched him stop just outside the door and look up and down the street. Fresh from the saloon, checking out the action.

'Shark,' Lonnie said.

June looked up at him.

'What we used to call lawmen who'd get a wild hair up their butt, go off on some crusade of their own.'

'Has that feeling to it, doesn't it?' I said.

'I'll be checking in with the Fort Worth PD, naturally,' Lonnie said.

'Naturally.'

Back in prison, when I was working on my degree, an instructor by the name of Cyril Fullerton took an interest in me, no idea why. It started off slowly, an extra comment on a paper I'd written, a note scribbled at the end of a test, but over time developed into a separate, parallel correspondence that went on through those last years, threading them together. Once I was out, we met, at a downtown diner rich with the smell of pancake syrup, hot grease, and aftershave. Cy had helped me set up a practice of sorts, referring an overflow patient or two to me and coercing colleagues to do the same, but, for all the times we'd made plans on getting together, something always came up.

We talked about that as a waitress named Bea with improbably red hair refilled our coffee cups again and again, how transparent it was that we'd both been finding a multitude of reasons not to get together, and later about how we were both bound to be disappointed, since over time we'd built up these images of the other and the puzzle piece before us didn't fit the place we'd cut out for it. At the time, new convert that I was, I thought we were speaking heart to heart, two people who understood the ways of the world and how it worked, their own shifts and feints included. Now I recognize the shoptalk for what it was: a blind, safe refuge, something we could hide behind.

We never met again. He was too busy, I was too busy. Gradually our feeble efforts to remain in touch faded away. But as it turned out, everything wasn't bluster, blinds, and baffles that day; Cy said something that has stayed with me.

'The past,' he said, resting three fingers across the mouth of his cup to keep Bea from pouring yet another re-fill, 'is a gravity. It holds you to the earth, but it also keeps pulling you down, trying, like the earth itself, to reclaim you. And the future, always looking that direction, planning, anticipating – that's a kind of freefall, your feet have left the ground, you're just floating there, floating where there is no there.'

CHAPTER FIVE

I'D LEFT ELDON plucking disconsolately at his banjo and humming tunelessly, the occasional word – *shadow, shawl, willow* – breaking to the surface. Breaking, too, onto disturbing memories of Val doing much the same. Pull the bike around back, I'd told him, and don't leave the place.

He'd been playing a coffeehouse in Arlington, Texas, near the university campus. After the gig, this guy came up to him to say how much he liked the way he played. They went out for a beer – Eldon was drinking by then – and, after that beer and an uncertain number of others were downed, to breakfast at a local late-night spot specializing in Swedish pancakes the waitress assembled at tableside. ('She folded them so gentle and easy, it looked like she was diapering a baby.') The guy, whose name was Steve Butler, told

Eldon he was welcome to crash at his house, that there was plenty of room and no one would be getting in anyone else's way. I'd been on the road for months, Eldon said, sleeping where I could, in parks and pullovers, behind unoccupied houses and stores; that sounded good.

First morning, he woke up with a young woman, Johanna, 'like in the Bob Dylan song,' beside him. Pretty much had her life story by the time I got my pants on, Eldon said. Butler, he discovered, was a lawyer who liked artistic types. People came and went in the house all day and night, some sleeping there, others just passing through. Johanna had staggered in around daylight, found space in a bed, and claimed it.

Second morning, Eldon woke to find his guitar, the old Stella he'd bought up in Memphis before he left, gone. Luckily he had the banjo stashed. Butler first insisted on paying for the guitar, then decided instead to buy him a new Santa Cruz as replacement, but Eldon never got it.

That was because on the third morning, Eldon woke up to find an empty house. He'd played at a bar that evening and remembered thinking how quiet the house was when he got back, but it had been past three in the morning and he was dead. Dead tired – not dead like the body he found in the kitchen when he dragged himself out there around ten a.m. hoping for coffee.

It was over by the refrigerator, where it had clawed a trench in the shingled layers of postcards, shopping lists, clipped cartoons, photographs, playbills, and magnets on its way down. The handle of a knife, not a kitchen knife but an oversize pocketknife or a hunting knife from the look, protruded from its back. There was blood beneath, but surprisingly little.

It was no one he'd seen before.

Eldon was pretty sure.

He'd been in the bar, playing country music, and he was in the right town for it, no doubt about that, all night. People kept buying him drinks. Figured he'd sung 'Milk Cow Blues' four or five times. Maybe more – he didn't remember much of the last set.

He'd called 911, patiently answered and reanswered the police's questions for hours even though he had precious little to tell them, and while there was no evidence aside from Eldon's presence there, the fit – musician, itinerant, obvious freeloader, alcohol on his breath and squeezing out his pores ('Not to mention black,' I added) – was too good for the cops to pass up.

Next morning, Steve Butler, who had been out of town at a family-law conference, showed up to arrange bail and release. Still couldn't get back in his house, he said. Eldon had shaken hands with him outside the police station, walked to his bike, and skedaddled. 'Not a word I've used before,' he said, 'but given the circumstances, Texas, lawmen on my trail, out of town by sundown, it does seem appropriate.'

Once Officer Baxter had left, as well as Lonnie, saying he'd make the calls to Texas from home, I sat thinking about the previous night as I dialed Cahoma County Hospital and waited for a report on Billy, a wait lengthy enough that I replayed our conversation, Eldon's and mine, twice in my head. The nurse who eventually came on snapped 'Yes?' then immediately apologized, explaining that they were, as usual, understaffed and, *un*usually, near capacity with critical and near-critical patients.

'I'm calling about one of those,' I said, giving her Billy's name and identifying myself.

He was doing well, I was told, all things considered. He'd gone through surgery without incident, remained in ICU. Still a possibility of cervical fracture, though X-rays hadn't been conclusive and the nearest CAT scan was up in Memphis. They were keeping him down – sedated, she explained – for the time being, give the body time to rebound from trauma.

I thanked her and asked that the office be called if there were any change. She said she'd make a note of it on the front of the chart.

And I sat there thinking – as June asked if it would be all right with me if she went out for a while, as Daryl Cooper's glass-packed '48 Ford blatted by outside, as a face and cupped hand came close to the single window that was left. Frangible, Doc had said. And who would know better? He'd seen one generation and much of another come and go. Delivered most of the latter himself.

What I was thinking about was death, how long it can take someone to die.

Back in prison, there was this kid, Danny Boy everyone called him, who, his third or fourth month, became intent upon killing himself. Tried a flyer off the second tier but only managed to fracture one hip and the other leg so that he Igor-walked the brief rest of his life. Tore into his wrist with a whittled-down toothbrush handle, but like so many others went cross instead of lengthwise and succeeded only in winning himself a week at the county hospital cuffed to the bed and in adding another layer to a decade of stains on the mattress in his cell.

Next six months, Danny Boy got it together, or so everyone thought. Stayed out of the way of the bulls and badgers, which is ninety percent of doing good time, spent days in the library, volunteered for work details. Worked his way up from KP to library cart to cleaning crew. Then just after dawn one Saturday morning Danny Boy drank a quart or so of stuff he'd mixed up: cleaners, solvents, bleach, who knows what else.

The caustic chemicals ate through his esophagus then on into his trachea before burning out most of his stomach; what they didn't get on the first pass, they got a second chance at on the reflux.

He spent eight days dying. They didn't bother to export him this time, since the prison doctor said there was nothing anyone could do, they might as well keep him in the infirmary. He'd be gone within twenty-four hours, the doctor said. Then stood there shaking his head all week saying, The young ones, the healthy ones, they always go the hardest.

They had him on a breathing machine that, with its two pressure gauges and flattened, triangular shape, looked like an insect's head. And he was pumped full of painkillers, of course. A lot of us went up there to see him. Some because it was different, it was a new thing, and anything that broke through the crust of our days was desirable; some to be relieved it wasn't them; probably others to wish, in some poorly lit corner of their heart, that it were. I went because I didn't understand how someone could want to die. I'd been through a lot by then, the war, the streets, nineteen months of prison, but that, someone wanting to die, was unimaginable to me. I wanted to understand. And I guess I must have thought that looking down at what was left of Danny Boy somehow would help me understand.

That was the beginning. Fast forward, zero to sixty in, oh, about six years, and I'm sitting in an office in Memphis listening to Charley Call-Me-CC Cooper.

The curtains at the open window are not moving, and it's an early fall day so humid that you could wring water out of them. Even the walls seem to be sweating.

'Before I was dead, before I came here,' CC is saying, 'I was an enthusiast, a supporter. I voted. I mowed, and kept the grass trimmed away from the curb at streetside. I kept my appointments. My garbage went out on the morning the truck came. My coffeemaker was cleaned daily.' He pauses, as though to replay it in his mind. 'You, the living, are so endlessly fascinating. Your habits, about which you never think, your cattle calls as you crowd together for warmth, the way you stare into darkness all your lives and never see it.'

CC believed himself to be a machine. Not the first of my patients with such a belief – I'd had two or three others – but the first to verbalize it. This was in the days before they became clients, back when we still called them patients, back before everything, the news, education, art of every sort, got turned into mere consumer goods. And truth to tell (though it would be some time before I realized this), the therapeutic tools we were given to treat them more or less took the patients as machines as well, simple mechanisms to be repaired: install the right switch, talk out a bad connection, find the proper solvent, and they'd take off across the floor again, bells and whistles fully functional.

I never knew what became of CC. He was a referral from a friend of Cy's who was giving up his practice to teach, and among the earliest of the deeply troubled patients who would become my mainstay. We had half a dozen sessions, he called to cancel the next one, pulled a no-show two weeks running, and that was it. Nothing unusual there; the attrition rate is understandably high. You always wonder if and how you could have done more, of course. But if you're to survive you learn to let it go. Couple of months after, I got a card from him, a tourist's postcard for some place in Kansas. Wheat fields, a barn, windmill, an ancient truck. He'd drawn in the Tin Man sitting astride the barn roof and written on the back, *Whichever way the wind blows!* Still later, around year's end, I got another. This one was plain, no location, just a photo of a white rabbit almost invisible against a snow-covered hillside. On the back he'd written, *I'm thinking seriously about coming back*, and underlined it. To Memphis? To sessions? To the living? I never knew.

The face at the window and the hand belonging to it, as it turned out, were those of Isaiah Stillman, on one of his rare forays into town. And looking uncomfortable for it, I first thought, but then, I don't believe Isaiah has ever looked uncomfortable anywhere. It was something else.

'Well . . .' I said.

'As well as can be expected.' He smiled. 'And you? It's been too long, Sheriff.'

'Not for much longer.' I gave him a second, then told him what had happened with Billy, and that Lonnie was back.

'Meaning that you'll be getting out from under.'

'Right.'

'Assuming that you *want* to get out from under.'

He sat – not in a chair, but on the edge of Don Lee's desk next to mine. He was wearing jeans, a white shirt tucked in, the fabric-and-rubber sandals he wore all the time, summer, winter, in between.

'The boy going to be okay?' he said. Isaiah had maybe twelve, fourteen years on 'the boy.'

'We're waiting to see.'

'We always are, aren't we? That's what we do.'

'Meanwhile, what brings you to town?'

'Oh, the usual. Flour, salt, coffee. Get a new wheel on the buckboard.'

'Miss Kitty'll be glad to see you.'

'Always.'

Isaiah and his group had arrived quietly, moved into an old hunting cabin up in the hills a couple hours from town, all of them refugees of a sort, he'd said. When I asked him refugees from what, he laughed and quoted Marlon Brando in *The Wild Ones*: 'What do you have?' Some local kids had got themselves tanked up and destroyed the camp. Rape and pillage

– without the rape, as Isaiah put it. Spearheaded by June, the town had pulled together and built a replacement camp, a compound, really: two thirty-foot cabins, a storage shed, a common hall for cooking and eating.

'Saw June down the street. She's looking good.'

I nodded.

'You too.'

'You know, Isaiah, in three years plus, I don't believe you've ever been in this office before.'

'True.'

'So what can I do for you?'

He started as someone banged hard on the plywood outside, once, twice, then a third time. We both looked to the window, where half a head with almost white hair showed above the sill. Les Taylor's son Leon. Deaf, he was always beating on walls, cars, tree trunks, school desks, his rib cage. Because the vibrations, we figured, were as close as he could get to the sound the rest of us all swam in.

'You understand,' Isaiah said, 'that it is very difficult for me to ask for help.'

I did.

'Back not long after we first came here, one of us—'

It had been only a few years; even my aging, battered memory was good for the trip. 'Kevin,' I said. He'd been killed by my neighbor Nathan's hunting dog. That was when we first found out about the colony.

Isaiah nodded. 'For some, like Kevin, the fit's not good. They drift away, leave and come back. Or you just get up one morning and they're not there. Not that they are necessarily any more troubled than the rest. It's . . .' He glanced at the window, where Leon was up on tiptoe looking in, and waved. 'It's like specific hunger – pregnant women who eat plaster off the walls because their body needs calcium and tells them so, even when they've no idea why they're doing it. Whatever it is these people need when they find their way to us, we don't seem to have it, and eventually, on some level or another, they come to that realization. Usually that's it. But not always.'

Pulling Don Lee's rolling chair close with his foot, he sank into it.

'This, what we have here, is . . . kind of the second edition? My first go at something like it was wholly unintentional. I was living with a friend, a critical-care nurse, in an old house out in the country, this was back in Iowa, and weekends we'd have other friends string in from all around, Cedar Rapids, Des Moines, Moline, even Chicago. Sometimes they wouldn't leave when Sunday night came, they'd stay over a day or two. Some of the stays got longer and, with the house an old farmhouse, there was plenty of room. One day Merle and I looked around and the thought hit both of us at the same time: We've got something here. By then, anywhere from half a dozen to a dozen people were resident or next door to being so.

'But things change, things that just happen, once you begin paying attention to them. People who've always been perfectly happy cooking up pots of spaghetti aren't around when dinnertime comes, Joanie's bread goes stale and gets fed to birds, people stay in their rooms, wander off into town . . . It was all over the space of six months or so. Toward the end, Merle and I were sitting outside in the sun one afternoon. He asked if I'd like a refill on iced tea, poured it, and handed it to me. 'Not working out quite the way we hoped, the way we saw it, is it?' he said. It was going to take a while, I said. He was quiet for moments, then told me he had a job over in Indiana, at the university hospital there, and would be leaving soon.

'Thing is, I wasn't so much upset that he was leaving as I was that he'd done it all, the planning, applying, without telling me. You've kept yourself pretty damn busy, he replied when I voiced that. And I'd already started to say, "Yes, building the . . ." when I realized that, first, I wasn't building anything, and second, I didn't even know what it was I'd thought I was building.'

This wasn't quite the same story I'd heard a couple

of years back, but storytellers do that. We all do, memories shifting and scrunching up to fit the story we want to tell, the story we want to believe. And maybe it's enough that the teller believes the story as he tells it.

'That's the long of it,' Isaiah said just as the phone rang. Red Wilson, complaining about his neighbor's barking dog. Red had recently moved into town after seventy-odd years on the farm. City life, he wanted me to know, was gettin' on the one nerve he had left.

'And the short?' I asked Isaiah after assuring Red I'd be out his way later that afternoon and hanging up the phone.

'There was a period when we didn't, but following that, Merle and I kept up over the years. He knew what we were doing here and kept saying he wanted to come see it for himself. Three months ago he set a date. When he didn't show up as planned, I thought, Well, something's come up at the hospital. Or, he was always driving these junker cars that gave out on him at the worst possible moment – maybe that was it. No response to my e-mails. I even tried calling, home and hospital both, but he wasn't either place.

'Yesterday, I finally found him,' Isaiah said. 'He was killed two weeks ago on his way here. In Memphis.'

CHAPTER SIX

SOME NIGHTS the wind comes up slowly and begins to catch in the trees, first here, then there, such that you'd swear invisible birds were flitting among them.

The dreams began not long after Val's death. I was in a city, always a city, walking. Sometimes it looked like Memphis, other times Chicago or Dallas. There was never any sense of danger, and I never seemed to have any particular destination to reach or any timetable for doing so, but I was lost nonetheless. Street signs made no sense to me, it was the dead of night, and no one else was around, not even cars, though I would see their lights in the distance, lashing about like the antennae of dark-shrouded insects.

I'd wake to the trees moving gently outside my windows and often as not go stand out among them.

As I was now.

Watching a bat's shadow dart across a moonlit patch of ground and thinking of Val and of something else she'd told me, something Robert Frost had said, I think: 'We get truth like a man trying to drink at a hydrant.'

My to-do list just went on getting longer. Go see Red Wilson about the barking dog. Get up to Hazelwood to interview Miss Chorley, former owner of Billy's Buick, to try to figure out what had been going on with him. Check in with MPD about Isaiah's friend Merle. Do whatever it was I was going to do to help Eldon.

I'd told Isaiah I would see what I could find out about his friend, and asked for a favor in return. 'Absolutely,' he said. 'Anything.'

So Eldon was up there in the hills with Isaiah and the others, where he should be safe until I figured out what to do.

Of course, I'd been waiting all my life to figure out what to do.

Back in prison it was never quiet. Always the sounds of toilets flushing, twittery transistor radios, coughs and farts and muffled crying, the screech of metal on metal. You learned to shut it out, didn't hear it most times, then suddenly one night it would break in on you anew and you'd lie there listening, waiting – not waiting *for* something, simply waiting. Just as I'd sat out on this porch night after night once Val was gone.

Like nations, individuals come to be ruled by their self-narratives, narratives that accrue from failures as much as from success, and that harden over time into images the individual believes unassailable. Identity and symbology fuse. And threats when they come aren't merely physical, they're ontological, challenging the narrative itself, suggesting that it may be false. They strike at the individual's very identity. The narrative has become an objective in its own right – one that must be reclaimed at all costs.

I thought about the radical shifts in my own self-narratives over the years. And I had to wonder what scripts might be unscrolling in Eldon's head now.

Or in Jed Baxter's, to fuel his pursuit of Eldon.

Whether by heritage, choice, or pure chance, we find something that works for us – amassing money, playing jazz piano, or helping others, it doesn't much matter what – and we hang on, we ride that thing for all it's worth. The problem is that at some point, for many of us, it stops working. Those who notice that it's stopped working have a window, a way out. The others, who fail to notice, who go on trying to ride – it closes around them, like a wing casing. It wears them.

I sat on the edge of the porch floor. A sphinx moth had landed in a swath of moonlight on the beam beside me.

Back in country, some of the guys would keep insects

in these cages they lashed together out of splinters of bamboo. Scorpions, a few of them, but mostly it was insects. Cockroaches, grasshoppers, and the like. They'd feed them, rattle them hard against the sides of their cages, jab them with thorns, talk to them. One kid had a sphinx moth he'd stuffed – with what, we never knew, but it was a raunchily amateur job, and the thing looked like one of the creatures-gone-wrong out of a bad horror movie. 'Just think,' he'd say, 'it'll never leave me, never die, never break my heart.' But the kid died, snipered while out on a routine patrol near the closest friendly village. Later that day Bailey brought the cage into the mess tent. He was sergeant, but no one called him that, and he had maybe a year or two on the kid. He set the cage on the table and stared at it as he slowly drank two cups of coffee. Then he picked up the cage, put it on the ground, and stomped it flat. His boots were rotting, like all of ours were (just as the French had tried to tell us), and like the feet inside them. A chunk of blackish leather fell off and stayed there beside the remains of the kid's cage as Bailey took his cup over to the bin.

CHAPTER SEVEN

TWO DAYS LATER, a cloud-enshrouded, bitter-cold Thursday, I was sitting in a Memphis squad room being lectured, basically, on what cat could piss on what doorstep.

I looked around, at the corkboard with its neat rows of Post-it notes, the ceramic-framed photo of a family from some fifties TV show, and the diploma awarded by Southwestern, as Sergeant Van Zandt wound down from his sermon on jurisdiction and proper channels. His wasn't all that different in kind from the sermons with which I'd grown up courtesy of Brother Douglas and successors back home among First Baptist's stained-glass windows, polished hardwood pews, and book-thick red carpeting. As kids, strung out by an hour of Sunday school followed by another hour or more of church service, my brother and I staged our own versions of such sermons over Sunday dinner, Woody preaching, me by turns amening, egging him on, and falling out with rapture. Pressed by our mother, Dad would eventually succumb and send us from the table.

'Nice cubicle,' I said when Van Zandt stopped to refill his lungs and drink the coffee that had gone lukewarm during his hearty polemic. 'What is it, MPD's finally got so top-heavy with management that they've run out of offices?'

Sometimes you just can't help yourself.

Tracy Caulding's glance toward me and half smile said the rest: Always more generals, never enough soldiers.

Tracy, mind you, was no longer on the force, she was now, God help her, a clinical psychologist, but she'd kept her hand in. She was one of the ones the department called on to counsel officers and evaluate suspects. And she was the one I called when I first hit Memphis.

The M.A. in social work she'd been working on when we met turned out not to be a good fit. She'd figuratively gone in the front door of her first job, she said, and right out the back one, back to school. To me she seemed one of those people who skip across the surface of their lives, never touching down for long, forever changing, a bright stone surging up into air and sunlight again and again.

We'd met for breakfast at a place called Tony Weezil's to catch up over plates of greasy eggs and watery grits before breaching the cop house to submit to further abuse. Tony Weezil's served only breakfast, opening at six and shutting down at eleven. After all, Tracy said, lifting a wedge of egg with her fork to let equal measures of uncooked egg white and brown grease find their way back to the plate, you've got one thing down perfectly, why mess with it.

She was telling me about a conference she'd attended, 'What Is Normal?' with authorities from all over delivering talks on Identity and Individuation, The Social Con Tract, Passing as Human, The Man Who Fell to Earth and Got Right Back Up. Some seriously weird people hanging around the hotel, she said – some of the weirdest of them giving the lectures.

'You miss it?' she said as the waitress, an anemic-looking thirtyish woman dressed all in pink, refilled our coffee cups.

'Why would I?'

'Not the professional stuff, the trappings. But the patients. Talking to so many different kinds of people, getting to know them on that level.'

'I'm not sure I did, in any real sense. There's this kind of call-and-response involved—'

'You hear what you listen for.'

'Right. And they figure out their side of it, what *they're* supposed to say. The good ones catch on right away, the others take a while. But sooner or later they all get there.'

She poured milk into her coffee, which she had not done with the first two cups, and absentmindedly watched it curdle. I signaled the waitress, who brought another of the small stainless steel pitchers, the same ones they used for pancake syrup.

'Maybe I'll reach that point,' Tracy said. 'You did try to warn me about social work, after all.'

'And like most warnings—'

'Exactly. But for now I like what I'm doing. I believe in it.'

What she was doing, aside from the consultations, was working with disturbed children. 'Troubled teens,' she had said. 'Put it that way, it sounds like something out of Andy Griffith, they'd meet in the church basement, have cupcakes, and talk about how no one likes them. When what *we're* talking about is kids who torture and kill the family pet, lock parents in basements, set fire to the house. I had one last month. Thirteen. A cutter. Couldn't get her to say a thing the whole hour – not that that's a big surprise. But then when she gets up to leave she says, "What's the big deal? It's just another cunt, that's all. I'm just opening it for them."'

Tracy had a warning of her own for me, about the gauntlet I'd be running. It would start with Sergeant Christopher Van Zandt, a man so devoutly incompetent that a new position had been created expressly to keep him—

'Out of harm's way?' I ventured.

'Out of the department's way.'

He was, she said, continuing education and informations officer.

'And whose nephew?'

'We're not quite sure. But he is a man in love with the sound of his voice, and no subject has yet been broached, be it deciduous trees or Polynesian dances, about which he did not know everything there was to know.'

'I believe we've met.'

'I'm sure you have.' She smiled. 'Many times.'

As I said, sometimes you just can't help yourself. With my remark about management, Van Zandt's locution ratcheted up a notch or two, tiny *b*'s exploding in the air directly before his lips, *t*'s clipped as though by shears. Complex sentences, dependent clauses, dramatic pauses – the whole nine yards.

Finally, having survived the sally, not to mention those *b*'s, we were passed along to someone who actually knew something. About the situation, that is.

'I suspect we won't be seeing one another again,' Sergeant Van Zandt said in the last moments, to make it clear we were done. He stood and extended his hand. 'It's been a pleasure.'

I looked at him closely. There were two people shut away in there, each with only a nodding acquaintance of the other.

We found George Gibbs in the break room staring into a cup of coffee as though everything might become clear once he reached the bottom. Periodically sweaty officers walked through from the workout room adjacent. Gibbs's mug was flecked with tiny paste-on flags and read WORLD'S BEST DAD. A gift from his kids, he told us – two weeks before his wife packed up and moved them all off to Gary-fucking-Indiana.

George, it seems, played bass with country bands, which had become increasingly a cornerstone for the friction between them, standing in for all the other things that went wrong and unspoken. 'Ain't no self-respecting black man alive that would play that shitkicker music,' his wife kept telling him. At least he didn't have to listen to that anymore, he said. Hell, country music was what he *liked*.

George Gibbs had sixteen years in, Tracy had told me. He was solid, looked up to by almost everyone, a man no one on the force would hesitate to trust with his or her life.

I told him about Eldon and his music, and he laughed.

'Banjo! Now that does beat all.'

George had responded to the call about Isaiah's friend Merle. Owner of a used-furniture store was unlocking his store that morning, caught a glimpse in the window glass alongside, went across the street to look. A body. Smack in front of the old paint store and half a block or so down from a bar, The Roundup, that was about the only thing open around there at night.

'Near as we can tell,' Gibbs said, 'he stopped to ask directions. Easy to get lost that side of town. Get caught up in there, everything looks the same – and there was a map half folded on the passenger-side seat . . . You know how it is: Maybe someone'll get wasted in The Roundup and start talking and that'll get back to us, but probably not. And maybe it didn't have anything to do with The Roundup. I could pull the report for you.'

'Taken care of,' Tracy told him.

'You read it?'

'Not yet,' I said. 'Wanted to hear you out first.'

Gibbs nodded. Approvingly, I thought. 'He was stabbed three, four times. With a small knife, probably just a ordinary pocketknife. ME thinks the first one was in the neck, of all places. Then the chest twice, maybe three times.'

'Wallet?'

'Gone. Got to us a day or so later, some kids who'd found it in a doorway, brought it in thinking there might be a reward. No money. Didn't look like anything else was taken.'

'But they left the car.'

'And the keys, right there by him. Thing is, he was a while dying. Small knife, like I said, and done quickly, more like punches than stabs. Shouldn't have killed him. But somehow or another, with one of the chest wounds, a major vessel got snagged. Blood wasn't pouring out, but it was coming strong. We found him, he was slumped against the side of the building with shoelaces tied around his thighs. He'd strapped his coat to his chest, by the wound, with his belt.'

'He was a nurse, he knew what was happening to him. Trying to keep himself alive until help arrived.'

'What the ME figured.' Gibbs finished his coffee and glanced into the empty cup. The answer wasn't there. Just like the help Merle had waited for.

'That it?' Tracy said once we'd thanked Gibbs and stepped back into the hallway. Its walls were paved with bulletin boards. 'You heading back home?'

I'd filled her in on the situation with Eldon; she knew I was.

'Then maybe you could do the department a favor,' she said.

Outside the property and evidence room in the basement, she spoke briefly to the officer in charge, who handed a clipboard across the half door. She signed and passed it to me, along with her pen. Officer Wakoski looked at the signatures, walked away into the maze of ceiling-high shelves, and returned with a package about six inches by nine.

'I'm pretty sure this isn't what Van Zandt had in mind,' I said.

'Probably not. But Sam Hamill did.' My old friend, now an MPD watch commander. He'd have sent the release through earlier.

The package was wrapped in plain white paper and heavy twine. Originally the knot on the twine had been sealed with wax, as on old letters, but the seal had been broken – when MPD opened it to check contents, I assumed. The front, in arching, thick cursive reminiscent of overdrawn eyebrows, read: FOR ISAIAH.

CHAPTER EIGHT

AS I RODE BACK toward home, along the river for a time before swinging inland, I watched a sky like old-time saddle shoes: horizon bright right up to the curving border where all went suddenly dark. It had been a season for storms. I remembered my grandfather's storm cellar, bare earthen walls, doors thick as tables with brackets into which you'd swing a two-by-four to close them, wood shelves sagging beneath the weight of water jugs, canned food, lanterns, and fuel. We'd all go down in there as the winds began, sit listening to them howl. As a kid I always expected the world to be new, fresh, changed all for the better, when we came back up. By the time I was ten or so we had stopped joining Grandad and his new family in the cellar, rode out the winds like modern folk.

Only the insurance lights were on, one on Municipal's side, one on ours, when I pulled in at City Hall. I put Isaiah's package on my desk by a note from June asking me to call her. The *J* of her signature was drawn leaning to the right, toward the other letters, its crosspiece sheltering them. The exclamation point after *Call me* was a fat, balloonlike shape with a smiley face below.

'Billy's taken a turn for the worse,' she said without preamble upon hearing my voice. 'Something about a blood clot, and hemorrhage. Dad's on his way up to Memphis. Doc Oldham went with him. Milly's up there already.'

'I'm sorry, June. Are you okay?'

'I guess. Better get off the phone, though. In case Dad or the hospital calls? But one more thing—'

'Okay.'

'That detective from Fort Worth? He's still around, asking questions. Did a swing through town first, hit all the stores. Then he drove out to the bars and roadhouses. Dad thought maybe you might want to look into it. "Since Eldon is nowhere about," as he said. He left a note for you, top drawer of your desk.'

I locked Isaiah's package in our possessions safe, which just about anyone could open with determination and a state-of-the-art nail file, and read the note from Lonnie, which told me, among other things, that Officer Jed Baxter was staying at the Inn-a-While out by the highway. So I got back in the Jeep and made the longish drive.

It's a habit you never quite get rid of. You pull in and sit for a time, watching closely, sizing up activity and positions, before getting out.

Three cars ranging from three to a dozen years old, an SUV with Montana plates, and a beat-to-hell pickup, half Ford, half spare parts, occupied the parking lot, making it a landmark business day for the motel. The number was missing from the door on room 8, but with 7 to the left and 9 to the right, and a Camry with Texas plates out front, I managed to figure it out. The Camry was gold-colored and well used, with stains on the carpet and seats, but all of it clean, none of the usual detritus of fast-food wrappers, sacks, paper cups. Even the boxes in the backseat were neatly stacked.

Jed Baxter didn't look all that surprised when he answered the door in his boxer shorts and T-shirt.

'Sheriff.' He backed out of the door to give me room.

A bottle of bourbon stood on the bedside table. From the look of things, the two of them had been keeping close company. The TV was on, one car in pursuit of another against what was all too obviously a back-projected city, volume turned so low it could have been sound from the next room. Baxter had been ironing his pants atop a damp towel on the dresser surface. One leg was folded back on itself, like a cripple's. He unplugged the travel iron and, since he was there by it, snagged his drink.

'You've been rooting around town, asking questions.' I'd settled in on the wide window ledge. He sat on the bed. We were maybe a yard apart.

'What we do – right, Sheriff?' He shrugged. 'I wasn't trying to hide anything. News in a town this size, it's not likely to gather flies.'

'And I'm thinking you knew that; it was part of the plan. Maybe it *was* the plan.'

'Ah. The plan.' Baxter held up his empty glass and motioned with its toward the bottle, offering. Why not? Been a long day. He found another plastic cup in the bathroom, half filled it, and brought it over.

'We spoke with your people back in Fort Worth. Seems—'

'I'm on a leave of absence, Sheriff.'

'Okay. Not quite the way they put it, but close enough. Explains the lack of a warrant or any other paperwork. You're here, they were careful to point out – a number of times – in no official capacity.'

Baxter smiled.

'So,' I said.

'So?'

'So it begins to look personal.'

He took a long sip of his bourbon before responding. 'It is, but not the way you think. Back in town I definitely got the feeling that you weren't eager to help.'

'I had no information for you.'

'Come on, Sheriff. You were just shining me on, didn't even want to talk to me.'

'In which case, you acted in a manner that assured I would.'

'Yeah, well. I've been doing this a long time. Whatever works.'

'What do you have against Eldon Brown?'

Baxter shook his head. 'Not him. My concern is Ron Nabors, the detective who nailed him for it and wouldn't hear otherwise. Still won't, for that matter.'

'You have reason to believe this Nabors was involved?'

'Laziness and habit, more like.'

'But you're looking to what? Take him down?'

'Not going to happen. And not that I'd want to. But your friend had nothing to do with the murder, and Big Ron's gotten away with too much for too long. Hell, we all have.'

I was not only a psychologist of sorts, I was a cop who had seen some of the worst mankind had to offer and an ex-con who had been privy to society's best, gnarled efforts at greatheartedness and manipulation. Altruism gets handed to me, I'm automatically peeling back the label, looking to see what's underneath. But I didn't say anything.

Baxter held the bottle up and, when I shook my head, poured what remained into his cup.

'I just want this set right, Sheriff. Came here hoping I might persuade Eldon Brown to go back with me, turn himself in. Nothing more to it. This point, I'm not expecting a lot more from life. Small wins. Small rewards. And most of those for someone else.'

CHAPTER NINE

'A MAN IS SLUMPED against a tree trunk in the jungle,' Cy, my old mentor, said that one time we met, 'or the side of an overpass, or a building smack in the heart of ritzy downtown – and he's dying. What he's thinking is, I'll never be able to tell Gladys how much I loved her, now I won't even get to try. What do you say?'

'I'm there?'

'For the benefit of the exercise, you are.'

'I'm not your student anymore, Cy.'

'Habit. So tell me: What do you, as a trained professional, say?'

'I say . . .' I began, and foundered.

'Exactly. You don't say anything. You listen.' Cy got up to leave. 'And that's the most important thing I can ever tell you. A small, simple thing – like most great secrets. You just listen.'

Strange how, as we age, our lives turn to metaphor. Memories flood in often and with little provocation, to the point that everything starts to remind us of something else. We, our actions, our lives, become representational. We imagine that the world is deeper, richer; in fact, it is simply more abstract. We tell ourselves that now we pay attention only to what's important. But sadly, what's important turns out to be keeping our routine.

Much like the town back there behind us.

Billy, it turned out, was going to be okay. He'd thrown a major clot, but it lodged in a leg vein and they managed to excise it surgically before it hit lungs or heart. Lonnie's description of the procedure when I spoke to him on the phone just before we left made it sound a lot like pulling a worm out of its skin. Except for all the fancy tools, equipment, and degrees, of course.

And now Jed Baxter and I were hiking up-country through the heaviest growth, four or five hollows and a long hill or two away from Isaiah's colony. Morning sunlight fell at a slant through the trees, struck the ground, and slid away into undergrowth without much purchase. Bird calls everywhere, growing silent as we approached, starting up again behind us. The barky, lisping chatter of squirrels.

The colony was looking good. The townspeople did a great job rebuilding, and the kids had done an equally great follow-up. Kids – I still thought of them as that, though none of them were, and most hadn't been for some time. The old sign – HIER IST KEIN WARUM – was back up, over the common hall now. They'd left the scorched edges and glued the ragged crack running lengthwise down its middle. At the far end of the compound, they'd built a playground worthy of the swankest inner-city park: animal-shaped swings, treehouse, wooden jungle gym, tunnels made from crates, pint-size barn and corral. One of the colony's newer members had been a woodworker, custom stairways, door casings, and the like for a builder back in San Francisco. The swing in the shape of a horse bore an elaborate swirl of hand-carved mane; delicate whorls ran into its ears.

The group was having its morning meal outside at one of the tables. Moira spotted us first, lifting a hand high in what served as both alert and greeting. The others turned, Isaiah came to meet us just inside the clearing, and nothing would do, of course, but that we eat with them. Fresh-baked bread, elderberry preserves, a kind of farmer's cheese made (Moira signed, with one of the children interpreting) by curdling milk with lemon juice.

I'd told Baxter what to expect, but you could tell it was a reach for him, taking all this in, accepting it for what it was. After we'd finished eating, he and Eldon stood nearby playing horseshoes (horseshoes!

how long had it been since I'd seen horseshoes?) and talking. We had helped clear the table and attempted to help more, but Moira and the others held up hands and pushed us away in pantomime, mugging in mock terror as though we were an invading army. Isaiah and I sat beneath a pecan tree at a table splattered with dried bird shit. Isaiah wiped what he could of it away with his hand, then bent down to wipe his hand on grass. He'd come a long way for a city boy.

'It's his brother's diary, from the last days,' Isaiah said of the package I'd brought him. 'The only other person, besides me, that Merle was ever close to. Thomas was dying from cancer, this weird kind that doesn't metastasize but recurs. First time, they pulled a tumor out of his stomach that weighed eleven pounds. Called it Gertrude – and Merle sent a birth announcement instead of a get-well card. Everything fine, then a little over a year later it was back, bigger this time, with more organ involvement. With the fourth one, Thomas refused further surgery.'

Isaiah leaned back against the tree.

'Remember when I told you about my grandmother, how she was the start of all this? How I was with her there at the end? Well, it wasn't like that with Thomas and Merle. Merle wasn't there with him, he was three states away, trying to save a marriage that had been too far gone for far too long. He was at work when the call came. A patient was going bad, a transplant that came in an hour or so before. They insisted the call was urgent, so Merle took it. It was the hospice telling him that Thomas had died that morning. Merle thanked them for letting him know and went back to work just as a code was called on the transplant patient. He was in charge that day, and ran it.'

You just listen.

'Merle was never one to show emotion much. Part of that was what he did, part of it simply who he was. But Thomas's death hit him hard. He'd call some nights and we'd exchange three or four sentences the whole time, he'd just be there on the phone, six, eight hundred miles away.'

I had to ask; old habits die hard. 'How long ago was this?'

'Little over a year.'

'So he was still depressed?'

'Why do you ask?'

I hesitated. 'To all appearances he was coming here to give you the diary.'

'You think he was suicidal.'

'Why would he want you to have it now? Something that was so important to him. It's the sort of action that people take—'

'Yes. It is.' Isaiah pulled off the tree and sat straight again, his hand flat on the diary. 'But I don't know. We'll never know, will we?'

'Could he have been ill, like his brother? A premonition of some kind?'

Isaiah was silent. He picked up the diary and stood. 'Does it matter?' he said.

CHAPTER TEN

I HAD FAILED again to listen.

Eldon wanted to think it over, this turning-himself-in thing.

Jed Baxter was back in unmarked room 8 at the Inn-a-While.

And the dog that Red Wilson complained about had, as it turned out, good reason to be barking.

Late afternoon, I drove out that way. By the time I came around the curve, Red was standing at the mailbox waiting for me. Jerry Langston, who runs the rural mail route, told me that Red was there every day waiting to collect his mail in person, adding that 'Heard you coming' was all he ever said. Which is what Red said to me.

My questions about the dog didn't fare a lot better. If I'd been collecting syllables, I'd never have made my quota. The barking had been going on for three, four days now, I managed to discover, but as of yesterday it got worse. Old man over there had taken to beating the dog for it, he was pretty sure.

Old man. Though still hard and lean, Wilson himself was well along in his seventies. He pointed across the dirt road to a house that gave the impression of having begun as a porch, developed a middling ambition, and undergone mitosis.

I drove over. It hit me the minute I stepped out of the Jeep, but the smell's common enough in the country that I didn't pay undue attention. The property owner, Bob Vander, stood inside the screen door peering out. He'd probably been watching me across the way at Red's. We'd never met, but I knew of him. Around to the side of the house, tethered on a ragged length of clothesline wrapped several times around its legs, the dog barked away.

'You want to step out here a minute, Bob?' I asked, though evidently that was about the last thing he wanted to do. As for me, I was tired and damned irritable and had, I thought, far more important things to attend to. Phrases like 'Or I can come in there and get you' drifted unbidden to the surface of my mind.

He emerged, finally, standing with one hand still on the screen-door handle. In a kind of travesty of Sunday dress, he wore a pair of pants that had once been the lower portion of a navy blue suit, and a white shirt with areas gone so thin they looked like windows onto a pale pink world. A small woman or a girl stood inside, just back from the door, peering out as Bob had done. I told him I was here in response to a complaint, and what the complaint was.

'I know, I know.' Here, his expression insisted, was yet another instance of everything in life being out to confound him. 'I done what I could,' he said. 'Dog just suddenly took hard to barking. Barking's what dogs do.'

The dog snarled and bared teeth when I approached, but settled as I put my hand on its head. No more barking. It had a goodly portion of short-haired pointer mixed in with goodlier portions of other things, and was malnourished and severely dehydrated; you could make out each individual rib.

I cut the clothesline with my pocketknife. The dog looked up at me and went to the back of the house, where the stench was strongest. It reared up, put its front paws on the rotting wood, and began barking again. Nearby, an ax leaned against a tree. I took it, urged the dog aside, and sank the ax into the side of the house.

I was remembering stories my father told me, stories passed down from *his* father, about old-time fiddlers who got religion and put away their devil's instruments in the walls of their houses, where people found them a hundred years later.

'You can't—' Bob said, then, with the second blow, the smell hit us full on and a small arm fell out of the gap in the planking.

The child was around six years old. He'd crawled through one of the broken boards inside the house, got stuck inside the wall, and died there. He'd been in the wall about a week, the coroner judged.

'And you didn't notice? That he was missing?' I asked Bob at the time. We were standing by the Jeep, him in cuffs I'd managed to find in the glove compartment, waiting for the troopers who would run him up to County.

'Well, it did get kinda quiet there for a while.' He raised an eyebrow, which pulled the rest of his face into what may have been meant to register some emotion, though what emotion, I have no idea. 'Before the damn dog commenced barking.'

That night the storm that had been threatening finally hit. I stayed in town, no way I was going to try to get out to the cabin, even in the Jeep. Standing outside the office beneath the overhang, I listened to the rain pound down, so loud that it obliterated all other sound, so heavy that I couldn't see across the street. Periodically gusts of wind would blast down Main, sudden and forceful as cannon shot, lifting the rain momentarily to horizontal as they passed.

We never found out who the woman was. Around twenty years old, Doc Oldham estimated, and mute.

That last caused the coroner to take a second look. The child's vocal cords, he decided, were undeveloped. Perhaps he had been mute too, or had simply grown up without learning to speak. The woman's child? Or younger brother? She went to the state home. Bob Vander went from county lockup to prison, where, weeks later, his body was found among a hundred pounds or so of bedding in one of the cement-mixer-like dryers in the prison laundry.

Eldon, I'd left surrounded by the compound's children, plunking on his banjo and singing, of all things, old minstrel songs. I had to wonder what the kids could possibly make of 'That's Why They Call Me Shine.' And I had to wonder, too, how they were making out up there, in all this rain. Fierce as it was here, they'd be getting it far worse. Rain could come down off those hills and through those hollows like a mile-long hammer, all at once.

I went back in to brew my second pot of coffee. Earlier I'd dialed up the Internet connection, thinking I'd e-mail J. T. and see how she was doing back in Seattle since I hadn't heard from her lately, but I kept getting kicked off. So we weren't the only ones getting slammed. And now even the phone itself was out.

When I heard the door, I wondered who could possibly be out in this and why; and when, disentangling myself from memories, I turned, for a moment I couldn't speak or think, because for just that moment I had the impression – I was certain – that it was Val standing there.

Then June threw back the hood of her coat.

'I—' And that was as far as she got. As though simply making her way here had used up whatever small reserves she had remaining. She went down all at once, the way kids do, onto the floor, and sat. I pulled her up out of the water and into a chair with a cup of hot tea in front of her and, as wind roared down Main and rain beat at the roof, learned that Billy was dead.

CHAPTER ELEVEN

'I DIDN'T KNOW where to go,' June told me. 'I thought you – someone – might be here.'

She had barely pulled in the driveway after the trip home from Memphis, the last hour of it through the storm, when the call came. Everyone else was still up there. Her home phone was down, but she had service on her cell. A tree limb had gone through the window of her living room and rain was blowing in like a fury and – well, she couldn't stay there alone, she just couldn't. She didn't know exactly what happened. They were taking him for tests or treatments, something like that, and things went wrong.

He was being transported to X-ray for a scan, I learned from Lonnie two days later, and in the elevator, with a nurse and aide in attendance, began to have trouble breathing. The ambu bag didn't work properly when they tore it out of its packaging, and the nurse, a recent graduate, had failed to bring emergency drugs. By the time they reached the basement and the doors opened, with them shouting for help, Billy was in full arrest.

Lonnie and I were sitting at the diner, interrupted regularly by well-wishers offering sympathy, mumbled homilies, parables drawn from their own lives. At one point Mayor Sims came over, started to say something and teared up, then wordlessly picked up the check on the table there by us and took it to the register.

'People're always talking about closure,' Lonnie said, 'about putting things to rest, dealing with the past, moving on.' He looked out the window, where Jody Ragsdale's rebuilt Ford Galaxie had broken down yet again. Car looked great, but it also was beginning to look as though Jody should have put in a little more time on the engine rebuild and a little less on bodywork. 'Billy was gone a long time ago,' Lonnie said.

'I know.'

'You ever have the chance to get up that way and talk to the car's owner?'

'Yesterday.'

I'd driven up late morning, after helping with the basic digging-out. Though there was a lot of standing water, loads of debris all around, and a few downed trees, the storm hadn't hit near as bad outside town.

No cows in trees, no porcupine quills driven into stop signs.

The house was much as described, one of those you still find here and there in the Deep South, looming up suddenly like foundered ships from behind banks of black locust, maple, and pecan trees. You could see where Billy'd been at work – sanded patches, raw timber, braces made of two-by-fours – but it was still a mess. When I stepped onto the porch, the boards sagged alarmingly.

No sign of a doorbell. I knocked hard, then, getting no response, sidestepped to one of the tall, narrow windows flanking the door. Sheer curtains obscured the view, reminding me of scenes in old Hollywood movies shot through a lens smeared with Vaseline to soften the focus. But inside I could see objects scattered about the floor, an overturned table, a chair on its side.

The door was unlocked, and Miss Chorley lay breathing, but shallowly, against a back wall, where the base-board showed remnants of at least three colors and the hash marks of being repeatedly chewed by a dog or other small animal. She'd caught the flocked wallpaper with her fingernails as she went down, ripping a long thin swatch that now curled around her arm like ribbon on a gift.

Her eyes opened when I knelt to take her pulse and speak to her. She wasn't really there, but she was stable. No wounds, as far as I could tell, other than a few bruises, and no blood. I found the phone, dialed the operator, and had her route me to the locals. Explaining what had happened, I asked for an ambulance and a squad. Then I asked for Sergeant Haskell.

He was on duty, I was told, but out on a call. They'd radio and send him right over.

I spent the wait checking the scene and checking back on her in equal parts.

They had come in through the back door, which looked to have been locked since about the time Roosevelt took office, but whose frame was so rotten that a child could have pushed the door in with one finger. Whether they had just started tearing the place up, then been interrupted by her, or whether they'd gone about it as she lay there, was impossible to say, but they'd done a thorough job. Walls had been kicked in, upholstered furniture sliced open, floorboards pried loose. If I read the signs right, they'd started here and, growing progressively frustrated at not finding what they were looking for, moved into the other of the two habitable rooms, which served as her bedroom, then about the house at random. The damage got less focused, more savage, as it went on.

Haskell was there inside of thirty minutes, trailing the ambulance by ten, a small, compact, muscular man dressed in trim-looking khakis and seersucker sport coat and so soft-spoken that listeners instinctively leaned toward him. I told him about Billy and we walked the scene together as the ambulance personnel packed up equipment, paperwork, and Miss Chorley.

'Yeah,' Haskell said at the back door. 'That's pretty much it. Then they went out the way they came in.'

'There have to be tire tracks back there.' If not the brunt of the storm, Hazelwood had got its fair share of rain.

Haskell nodded. 'We'll get impressions. Most likely this was kids. And most likely the tracks—'

'Will match half the vehicles in the county.'

'Not our first rodeo, is it?' He went through to the porch to light a cigarette. Much of the floor had rotted through out here; each step was an act of faith. From beneath, three newborn kittens looked up at the huge bodies crossing their sky. 'Woman lives here all these years, no bother to anyone, you'd think she could at least be left alone. Sort of thing seems to be happening more and more.'

He shook his head.

'And it's just starting. Towns like ours get closer to the bone, less and less money around, jobs hard to come by – no way it's going to stop.'

We stood there as the ambulance pulled out. I looked down at the kittens, hoping their mother was not the cat I had seen dead and swollen doublesize beside the road on my way in.

'You figure they were looking for money?' Haskell said.

'Looking, anyway.'

He stepped off the porch to grind his cigarette out on bare ground. 'Kids . . .'

'Maybe not.'

I don't know why I said that. There was no reason to believe it was anything other. Just a feeling that came over me. Maybe I had some sense – with Billy's being up that way and coming back to town after so long, with his accident, with my finding the old lady like this – that we had ducks lining up, or as my grandfather would have said, one too many hogs at the trough.

Or maybe it was only that I wanted so badly for the things that happen to us to have meaning.

CHAPTER TWELVE

MOST OF THE TOWN, what was left of the town, came to Billy's funeral. Mayor Sims gave a eulogy that had to have set a record for the most clichés delivered in any three-minute period, Brother Davis prayed, preached, and strode about with one or both hands raised, and toward the end Doc Oldham let out a fart that made people jump in the pews; when they turned to look, he himself turned, staring in disapproval at widow Trachtenburg there beside him.

Throughout, Lonnie sat quietly inside his dark brown suit as though it might be holding him upright and in place. June kept looking up, to the ceiling, and down, at the floor – anywhere but into her father's or other eyes.

There had been another hard rain, though this time without the dramatics, and the cemetery outside town had gone to bog, pallbearers slipping on wet grass, mud halfway up shoes and over the top of some, folding chairs sinking leg by leg into the ground.

I spent the afternoon with Lonnie and the family. Greeted visitors, poured gallons of lemonade and iced tea, helped with the cleanup once the last stragglers strayed onto the front porch and away.

Afterward, Lonnie and I sat together on the porch. He'd brought out a bottle of bourbon, but neither of us had much of a taste for it. He was looking at the tongue-and-groove floor we'd spent most of a week putting down the summer before.

'Hell of a mess out here,' he said.

'In there, too.' So much mud had been tracked from the cemetery, the porch floor could have been of dirt rather than wood. Lonnie was still wearing his suit. It didn't look any fresher than he did.

He asked if I'd heard any more on the old lady, Miss Chorley, who was recovering but, from the look of things, headed for a nursing home.

'Lived on that land, in that house, all her life,' he said, 'and now she gets shipped off some place where they'll prop her up in front of the TV, dole out crackers or cookies every day at two o'clock, and cluck their tongues when she complains. No family, so the county will end up taking the house.'

He looked down again.

'Nothing right about it, Turner. Person gets through

even an average life here on this earth, never mind a long one – they deserve better. Sitting in some brightly lit place with powdered egg or applesauce running down your front, can't even decide for yourself when you're going to pee.'

I had nothing to say to that. He scuffed at the crust of dried mud there by his chair and after a moment asked, 'Staying in town again tonight?'

'Thought I'd head back home, see if it's still there.'

'Might want to take food, water, emergency supplies. A native guide.'

'Hey, I've got the Jeep. Which, now that I mention it, since you're back on the job, you should reclaim.'

'I'm *not* on the job, Turner. I don't want to be sheriff anymore. I'm not sure I want to be much of anything anymore. Other than left alone.'

After a moment I said, 'It will pass, Lonnie.'

'Will it? Does it?'

We had one quick hit off the bourbon there at the end. As at the accident scene, I didn't make the usual noises – Everything's going to be all right, If there's anything I can do – because it wasn't like that between Lonnie and me. Instead we just said good night. Lonnie stood on the porch, all but motionless, and watched as I drove away. The lights were already off inside the house.

My slog back up to the cabin proved worthy of a brief PBS documentary, complete with process shots of looming black hills closing in on the Jeep's tiny headlights and time-lapse photography of the hapless vehicle negotiating treacherous mudslides, but I made it. The whole time, I was thinking about settlers carving their way into this country for the first time, how hard, how damned near impossible, it had been. Even in my grandfather's time, most people were like birds that never strayed far from their birth tree; a trip of a hundred miles was a major undertaking.

As I came around the bend in the lake, I saw the shadowy figure sitting on my porch.

'You walked here?' I asked minutes later, metal popping behind me as the Jeep's engine cooled. My night, apparently, for conversations on porches.

'Waded is more like it.'

'And it looks like you brought about half the mountain with you.'

Eldon took off his shoes, stomped his feet hard against the porch floor, and we went inside. I motioned for the shoes and, when he handed them over, tossed them in the sink. Poured a shot for me from the bottle there on the counter, looked up at him. He nodded, so I got another glass. I heard a moan, starting low and rising in pitch, and glanced outside to see tree limbs on the move: Wind was building again.

'How are things at the camp?' I asked.

'Could have been worse. Minor injuries, some broken windows. About half the storage building got taken out by a tree. Lot of the stores, bulk flour and so on, are likely ruined.'

'But everyone's okay.'

'They're a tough bunch up there. Take more than a storm to throw them.'

I hauled myself bodily out of my thoughts, how I'd got to know the group, what they'd already been through both individually and collectively, to ask: 'Been waiting around long?'

'Not too long. Easy to lose track of time here. Few hours, I guess.'

'Then you have to be hungry.'

I pulled bread, sliced ham, pickles, mustard, and horseradish out of the refrigerator, put together a couple of sandwiches for us. Eldon had his down in about three bites. Then he grabbed the bottle off the counter and poured for us.

'I came here—'

'I know.'

He looked at me, utterly calm and not unduly surprised, but wondering.

'No other reason you'd be here.'

He nodded. 'I can't go back, John. My mind tells me I should, I know that's the smart thing to do, the only real solution. But something inside me, something as strong as all that logic and good sense, screams *No!* at the very notion.'

It struck me again, as it had so often in my time

as a therapist and in years since, how few of us actually make choices in our lives, how few of us *have* choices to make. So much is mapped out: in our DNA, our class and temperaments, the way we're raised, the influence of those we meet. And so much of the rest is sheer chance – where the currents take us. However much we believe or feign to believe that we're free agents, however we dress it up with debates on nature, nurture, socialization or destiny, that's what it comes down to.

'Where will you go?' I asked.

'Hey, the invisible man, right? *Dans la nuit tous les chats* and all that.'

'Or as Chandler said, "Be missing."'

'Exactly.'

'It won't be easy.'

'Not as easy as it used to be, for sure. Too many electronic fingers in too many pots now. But I've been half off the grid my whole life. This is just about pushing it a little further – a matter of degree.'

'They won't stop looking.'

'For the most part, they already have. The documents are out there – warrants, arrest record, and all that. They'll stay. But only as history, and just as immaterial.'

'You'll be out there as well, Eldon. A ghost. Nothing you can hold on to.'

'I know.' He smiled. 'I feel lighter already.'

'You should at least talk to—'

'Isaiah, yes. I had the same thought. Get the advice of an expert on the cracks and crawlspaces of society.'

'And?'

'We talked. I've been well advised. He's a remarkable person, John. They all are.' I had fetched a couple of blankets from the closet and thrown them to him; he'd settled under them on the couch. 'As, my friend, are you.' He peered out, Kilroy-like. 'There is no way I can ever say how much your friendship has meant to me.'

'There's no way you'd ever need to.'

When I got up the next morning, Eldon and bike were gone. The banjo case lay on the kitchen table. Eldon had scribbled a note on the back of a magazine I'd been intending to read for about a year now: *She always said that instruments don't belong to people, we just borrow them for a while.* I sat over coffee, thinking about when Eldon and I first met, about that time in the roadhouse out on State Road 41 when he'd refused to fight the drunk who'd smashed his guitar, about the music he and Val used to play together. About how much a man can lose and how much music he can make with what he has left.

I drove in to work to the accompaniment of a wide range of static on the radio, low bands to high, weather playing havoc with that the same as it was with everything else. Black and charcoal clouds hung just over the treetops. It was nine but in the half-light looked more like five, and as I scrabbled and slid along, gearing down, gearing up, momentarily I had the sensation of being underground.

CHAPTER THIRTEEN

THE DRIVE WAS FOLLOWED by an ordinary day in which, beginning the moment my feet hit the town's asphalt a little past ten, I dealt with:

Jed Baxter, who wanted to know where the hell Eldon had gone to;

Mayor Sims, who came bearing go-cups of coffee then casually got around to asking if it might be possible for 'the office' to do a background check on Miss Susan Craft up Elaine way;

Dolly Grunwald from the nursing home, brought in by one of her nurses, with the complaint that they were poisoning her out there;

and Leland Luckett, who parked his shiny new Honda out front of City Hall with the butt of the buzzard who'd flown into the windshield pointed to the door of our office. He'd just been driving along when the thing flew straight at him, right into the windshield. Like a damn missile, he said. It was quite a sight. Thing was the size of a turkey, and stuck in there so firmly that it took the two of us to pull it loose. I'm still not sure what else Leland thought I could do for him. In exasperation I finally asked if he thought my arresting the damn bird, dead as it was, would be a deterrent.

Afterward I walked across the street to the diner for coffee and a slice of What-the-hell pie. Most places would just call it Pie of the Day, something like that, but Jay and wife Margie took notice of how many people said 'Just a cup of coffee' only to add 'What the hell – a piece of pie, too.' Not surprisingly, since everyone had been watching out the front windows, most of the conversation was about Leland and his buzzard.

Margie came out from behind the counter to take my order and ask if I'd heard about Milly Bates. Everybody'd noticed how shaky she looked at Billy's funeral. Not just in pain or overwhelmed, Margie said; it was like you could see through her. Then this morning her folks'd gone over to check on her and she was gone. House wide open, no note, nothing.

'What about the car?' I asked.

'In the driveway. But it hadn't been running for weeks, someone said. The sheriff—' She stopped, realizing her blunder, embarrassed by it, but for me, not herself. 'Lonnie, I mean – is checking on it. Coffee?'

'Coffee.'

'And ... ?'

'Just coffee. To go.'

I drove out that way with the coffee in the cup holder on my dash. At some point the lid slipped and coffee sloshed over the dash and floorboard, and I barely noticed. I was busily trying to put things together in my head, things that in all likelihood didn't even belong together, a confused young man's death, an old woman who'd lost everything, now Milly.

Lonnie's car stood by the house with the driver's door open and its owner nowhere to be seen. It was his wife's car really, but after giving up the job and Jeep he'd 'taken to borrowing it,' and after close to a year of that, Shirley had gone out without saying a word to him and bought a new one just like it. The door to the house was open, too. Inside, flies shot back and forth like tiny buzz bombs, and I followed them to the kitchen where a table full of food brought around by neighbors and friends – a roasted chicken, casseroles, slices of ham, dinner rolls, cakes – sat mostly untouched. The coffeemaker was still on, with a few inches of coffee that looked like an oil spill; I turned it off. On the refrigerator alongside were a shopping list, discount coupons, a magnetic doll surrounded by clothing and accessories, also magnetic, and an old Valentine's Day card.

Lonnie spoke from behind me. 'Milly and me, we never saw much of each other.'

One thing about living in a town this size is, you pretty much know what goes on between people without it's ever being said. One thing about living these fifty-plus years and having a friend like Lonnie is that when it does get said, you know to keep quiet.

'Boy had a hard life,' Lonnie went on. 'Not making apologies, and I know he brought a lot of it on himself. But there wasn't much that was easy for him, such that you had to wonder what kept him going.'

I had been wondering that, ever since I could remember, about all of us.

'Milly married him, she took that trouble, Billy's trouble, to herself. And now . . .' He stared at flies buzzing into covers and containers, bouncing off, hitting again. 'Now, what?'

'You sure you want to be out here, Lonnie? Shouldn't you be home with Shirley?'

'Too much silence in that house, Turner. Too much . . .' He shook his head. 'Just too much.'

In my life I've known hundreds paralyzed, some by high expectations, others by grief or grievous wounds; finally there's little difference. That's where Lonnie was headed. But he wasn't quite there.

'Footprints out back,' he said. 'Two, three men. Cigarette stubs mashed into the mud.'

'Like they were there for a while.'

'Could just be friends ... Whatever tracks there were out front are mostly gone, from the rain. Took a look around back, though. Old soybean fields out that way. And someone's been in there recently, with what looks to have been a van, maybe a pickup.'

'No signs of a search, I guess.'

'Hard to say. Milly wasn't much of a housekeeper. Picking up Cheetos bags and wiping off counters with a damp rag being about the extent of it. Drawers and closet doors open, clothes left where they fell – all business as usual.'

'Speaking of which—'

'Clothes? No way to know. And no one close enough to be able to tell us.'

'So except for some tire tracks and a few cigarette butts that for all we know could have been a friend's, we have no indication that anything's amiss here. She could just have packed up and left.'

'Without warning, and with her entire family here.'

'People in stress don't plan ahead, Lonnie. They panic, they bottom out. They run.'

'Like Billy did.'

'As we all have, at some point.'

'True enough.' Stepping up to the kitchen table, he removed the clear plastic cover of a cake with white frosting. Flies began buzzing toward it – from the entire house, it seemed. 'In the bathroom. There's a bottle of antidepressants, recently refilled, and a diaphragm on the counter in there. How likely is it that she'd leave those behind?'

We went through the house room by room. No sign of purse or wallet. There were two suitcases, bought as a set and unused, smaller one still nestled inside the larger, in a closet. In the bedside table we found the checkbook, never balanced, and beside it, nestled among a Bible, old ballpoints and chewed-up pencils, Q-tips and hairpins, we found a cardboard box in which, until recently, a handgun had made its home.

CHAPTER FOURTEEN

I NEVER SAW Eldon again.

So many people come into our lives, become important, then are gone.

Back in college, back before the government jacked me out of my shoes to drop me in jungle boots that started rotting from day one, I had an astronomy professor who compared human relationships to binary stars endlessly circling one another, ever apart yet exchanging matter. Dr Rob Penny was given to fanciful explanations of the sort, amusing and embarrassing a classroom filled with freshmen there only because astronomy was the easy science credit. Planetary orbits, fractals and star systems, eclipses – all met with his signature version of the pathetic fallacy. Incipient meddler in others' lives that I was even then, I often wondered about Dr Penny's own relationships.

Lonnie was at State headquarters co-opting their resources to do what he could about finding Milly, June was up at the colony with a handful of townspeople (including, to everyone's astonishment, Brother Davis) helping them rebuild, and I was answering the phone.

Jed Baxter had been in earlier, spitting and chewing scenery and saying over and over that I just didn't get it, did I, telling me how he had come all this way expressly to give Eldon a chance, then telling me he was heading back to Fort Worth. For a moment – something in his eyes – I actually thought he was about to say 'back to God's country.'

So I was answering the phone, and everybody in town or nearby was on the other end. Wanting to know

what was going on with the sheriff's daughter-in-law,

if someone could come out and talk to the senior class about careers in law enforcement,

why people were up there in the hills helping those weirdos when their own town could use a good cleanup,

what we were going to do about daughter Sherri Anne who kept going off with that no 'count Strump boy,

what the old military base out by the county line was being used for, because they'd been seein' strange blue lights over that way late some nights, whether there was an ordinance against someone keeping pet snakes,

and again, off and on the whole day, what was going on with Milly, had we found her yet, they heard there was blood at the scene, we should check with her cousin in Hot Springs, did we know she'd been seen in the company of that Joseph Miller person who'd recently up and moved here from Ill-uh-noise.

Between calls I did some of the things I most dislike doing: checked invoices and bills, marking the ones June should pay; organized the papers on my desk into four piles every bit as confusing as the single pile had been; and read through our voluminous backlog of arrest records (there were two). When I looked up, Burl Stanton was about a yard away from my desk, standing quietly. I hadn't heard him come in. But then, I wouldn't.

Burl is our local career vet. Most every town has one or two of them. He reminded me of Al, the ex-soldier, ex-fiddle player I'd befriended as a child. Al worked in the icehouse until it closed, then lived mostly on the street. Burl hadn't lost near as much as Al, but after six years as a ranger, after all he'd seen, he had no further use for society. He just damn well wanted to be left alone, and this was one of the few places left in the country that, if you damn well wanted to be left alone, people damn well did. He had a shack out by the old gravel pit, but spent most of his time ranging through the hills.

'Two men,' Burl said. I waited. He wouldn't be here, in town, still less in this office, without good cause. And he had his own manner of talking, words alternately squeezed out and spurting, like water from old pipes. 'Tracked them.'

One of the men had been carrying the other – something Burl had seen a lot back in country, and what must have got his interest in the first place. He'd caught sight of them down one of the hollows, pulled back as they came up the hill, then fell in behind. The carried man was hurt bad, blood coming off him hard, and after a mile or so of stumbling along, barely staying afoot, the other one gave up, dumped him there. 'Kin show you,' Burl said. He'd lost interest at that point and backtracked the two men to where they'd started. They'd come a piece on that one man's two legs. All the way from the chrome-bedecked van where Burl found an unconscious woman. The van was lying on its side. 'Looked like it done played pinball with more than one tree,' Burl said. The woman was trapped partway beneath. He'd had to snap off a sapling, lever the van up with one hand, and reach in and get hold of her with the other. 'Don't think I hurt her much extra.'

Then Burl had fashioned a travois from saplings and vines and brought her all the way to town on it.

Dropped her at the hospital, but they kept asking him questions, so he came here. He didn't have no answers for them.

Doc Oldham and Dr Bill Wilford were standing alongside the gurney when I got there, each doing his level best to defer to the other. Finally, with a shrug, Doc went to work, Wilford assisting. The small ER reeked of fresh blood, alcohol, and disinfectant. One of the exam lights overhead flickered, as though the bulb were going bad. I remembered how field hospitals would be filled with the stench of feet shut up in boots for weeks, a smell so strong that it overpowered those of blood, sweat, chemicals, piss, and cooked flesh.

It was Milly. And it would be some time, Doc told me as he worked, before he'd know much of anything. Looked like a crushed chest, fractured hip, multiple compound fractures – for starts. Spine seemed intact, though. Lungs and heart good. Pressure down, but they were pumping fluids in as fast as they could. I might as well go about my business.

Outside, the day was bright, the air clear, giving no hint of devastations recently wrought, or of those to come.

I was able to get the Jeep within sight of the crash site. Burl sat beside me looking grim the whole time. He didn't care for motorized vehicles much more than he did for towns. Had too many of them shot out from under him back in the desert, he said.

The road was dirt, naturally, one of hundreds that crisscross these hills, and barely the width of the vehicle, with layer upon layer of deep-cut ruts and damn near as many recent washouts. Now, it was primarily mud. Their being up here, on a road like this, made no sense at all. And how they'd got as far as they did in that lame tank of theirs was anyone's guess.

The van was a glitz-and-glory Dodge, with enough chrome on it to look as though it might have escaped from some celebrity chef's TV kitchen. The sapling Burl used to free Milly was still there, half under the vehicle. Ants and other shoppers had found the blood. There were banners of duct tape on the front passenger seat. Doc had said much the same of Milly's clothing.

Most of the windshield was gone, the remains scattered about. I kicked at them, bent over, and picked up a floppy piece with a puncture surrounded by starring. So the shot had come from behind. Blood-and-meat splatter on the windshield fragments and on the dash where the insects were chowing down. I found the handgun eight or nine yards off, plunged into the ground muzzle-first as if planted there and just starting to grow.

The driver had been shot as the three of them slithered and slid along. With Milly taped into the passenger seat, apparently. Why? Why did they have her in the first place, why were they on this road that led essentially nowhere? And who made the shot? The half-buried handgun was a .38, same as the one that came out of Milly's bedside table. But Milly was in the passenger seat, and the shot had come from behind. What possible reason would the second man have had to shoot his driver partner? And if he did, why then would he sling the man across his back and try to carry him out?

Way, way too many questions.

Not to mention who the hell were these guys in the first place.

I looked around some more – as J. T. had discovered, it wasn't like city work, with crime-scene officers, an ME, half the police force, and maybe a coffee runner or two at your beck and call – and figured I'd best give State a call, have them come down and get a fix on this. With some reluctance Burl got back in the Jeep and directed me to the dead man. There were snails all over his face. Something, a dog most likely, had eaten four fingers.

Burl helped me roll the man in a tarp and load him in the back of the Jeep, then said he'd be heading out if I didn't need him for anything else. I thanked him for being a good citizen, and at that he laughed. Stood peering closely at me in that way he had, not blinking.

'Don't know what went down here,' he said. 'Don't much care. But a man dies, it needs to be marked.'

Simple sentiments divested of qualification or abstraction, plainly spoken – just as the speaker was out here attempting to lead an unabstracted life. It was foolishness, but it was a damned near heroic strain of foolishness,

Driving back I thought how, as Americans, there are mountain men or cowboys inside us all, Henry David Thoreau and Clint Eastwood riding double in our blood-streams and our dreams.

Always slow off the block, I didn't have my first tree house till I was fifteen. Just past the backyard, a hill swelled, partly cut away and thick with trees, a remnant of wilderness tucked into one far corner of our property, jutting out above the chicken-wire run where my father kept his bird dogs. I had his permission, and a stack of lumber from a feed shed he'd torn down a while back. Just watch for nails, he said.

For weeks I prepared. Took graph paper I hadn't used since fifth grade and drew up plans. Dad had passed along a number of his old tools; I put them, along with a tape measure heavy as an anvil, in the shoeshine box he'd built me when I was ten or so. Struggled up the hill with two or three planks or two-by-fours at the time and left them there in piles roughly sorted by length. Had the wheelbarrow up there too, complete with jelly jars of nails and brackets, a bunch of rags, a carpenter's level, and a spot for a pitcher of red Kool-Aid. I was ready.

I went up the hill Saturday morning at eight after scarfing down the oatmeal my mother insisted upon. In turn I insisted upon taking lunch, peanut butter and apple-jelly sandwiches, with me. Dad came up around noon to see how I was doing, then a few hours later to tell me I should think about coming on down, then finally to fetch me back to the house.

I was at it again, not long after daybreak, on Sunday. And for the next two weeks I was obsessed. Up there after school until dark, one night even talked Mom and Dad into letting me take along an old kerosene lantern and hang it from a limb. Put the frame and floor down three times before I got it plumb, planed and whittled at boards till they fit together for walls, corners had to be aligned just so. I pulled old nails and filled the holes, sawed off ends, sanded out rough spots.

The tree house was completed late Saturday afternoon. I'd even built in benches along two sides, and a tiny porch out front. I sat on that porch most of the rest of Saturday and Sunday.

After that I rarely went back. From time to time I'd idly climb the hill and check, watching as it slowly came apart. Years later, back from jungles half across the world and on a rare visit, I wandered up there after dinner and came upon it, surprised. I'd forgotten my tree house. Little was left, a few floorboards and fragments of wall, rusted nails in the trees. On one of the remaining boards a mockingbird had built its nest.

CHAPTER FIFTEEN

THEY'D STABILIZED MILLY, sent her on up to Memphis, Doc said. Out of our hands now. He'd been sitting on the bench outside the office when I returned. We watched as lights went off and stores got locked up and cars pulled out toward home. Except for the diner now, everything was deserted. Framed in its front windows, anonymous heads bent over burgers, steak platters, pie and coffee.

'But *damn*, that felt good. Can't tell you how I miss it, Turner.'

'Saving lives?'

Mind caught in memories, he was quiet a moment.

'Not really. It's more about knowing exactly what to do – the branching decisions you make, the way each decision, each change, calls up a sequence of actions – and doing it almost without conscious thought. Not much in the world that compares.'

Doc would have gone on, possibly for hours, but it was right about then that Jed Baxter pulled up in his Camry. I met him at the street.

'Back so soon? And please tell me that the passenger in your backseat is merely sleeping.'

'Damnedest thing,' Baxter said. 'Got a late start, so I figure what the hell, I'll grab lunch before heading out. And I stop at this mom-and-pop-looking place – out there right before you hit the highway?'

'Ko-Z Inn.'

'Right. Nasty food.'

'But filling.'

'Ought to be their motto . . . So, after five or six coffees at the café and half an hour on the road, naturally I gotta pee, so I pull over. Do my thing, and when I look up, this guy's come out of the trees and is climbing in my car. Time I get there, he's got his head down under the dash poking around at wires.' Baxter opened the back door. 'Figured I'd bring him to you.'

'Kind of a going-away present.'

'For the one that's staying, right. Hope he's okay. Had to thump the sucker twice to put him down.'

'Cuffs, huh?' Plastic, but police issue.

'Always carry some with me. Hey, you never know.'

'That right arm's not looking too good.'

'What can I say? Man didn't care to be cuffed. Laying there on the ground with his lights out, but he's still fighting at me.'

'And you had to thump him again.'

'Maybe. A little. You want the sonofabitch or not?'

Baxter and I hauled him in and laid him on the bunk in one of the cells. Doc sauntered in complaining that this didn't look to be much of a challenge, checked reflexes and pupils and the like, and said that in his hardly-ever-humble opinion the man was fit to be jailed.

Which left a couple of things hanging.

First off, since we had a prisoner, someone was going to have to hold down the fort tonight, which probably meant me.

Then there was the fact that this guy matched the description I'd got from Burl: medium height but looking taller because of being so thin, maybe 150, and what there was, muscle; hair light brown, long on the sides and back, not much left on top; blue-green Hawaiian shirt, heavy oxfords, khaki slacks.

So in all likelihood I had one of Milly's kidnappers (if that's what they were) and a killer (assuming that he shot his partner), all dressed up nice with his lights out, back in my cell. An enforcer of some kind? Runner? Or just hired help? I couldn't help but think how it turned out the last time something like this came along. I'd walked into the office to find June and Don on the floor unconscious, our prisoner gone. The fallout from that had rung in the air for some time, leaving behind a number of bodies, Val's included.

I called Don Lee to tell him what was going on, and that I'd take the night watch if he'd come in first thing in the morning. I sat there all night in the dead quiet drinking pot after pot of coffee, staring at the black window, and thinking about prison, how it was never quiet, how, surrounded by hundreds of others, you were as alone as it was possible to be.

But before that, I said good-bye again to Jed Baxter and rejoined Doc Oldham on the bench outside. The diner was closing for the night, Jay and Margie and Cook (the only name he'd admit to) making their final runs to the trash barrels in back. Pale rainbows shelled the few lights along the street, cyclones of flying insects pouring inexhaustibly into them.

'Sit here some days,' Doc said, 'and I half expect tumbleweed to come rolling down that street. Audie Murphy to ride in on his goddamn white horse. You know who Audie Murphy was?'

I did. Some of the first movies I remember seeing. Audie Murphy mugging and mumbling, Sergeant York doing turkey calls. All those grand films about war from a much younger, far more innocent nation, innocent not in the sense of guiltlessness but in that of immaturity, of callowness.

'We want so badly to believe things are simple, Turner. That good and evil are in constant battle and by Tuesday of next week one or the other will win. You've said the same yourself.'

'Many times.'

'And still—' He laughed, and had to catch his breath. 'And still we are not exempt.'

'No.'

We sat there quietly, beset by mosquitoes and the occasional errant moth. Cook emerged from the alley with his bicycle, mounted it, and rode off into darkness. Jay's truck pulled out and turned in the other direction. Once-bright red and yellow flames on the bicycle were mostly shadow. The truck's patches and layers of paint resembled, more than anything, fish scales; some were thick as artichoke leaves.

After a time, Doc said, 'You haven't told anyone, have you, Turner?'

'No.'

'Maybe you should.'

I was silent. Who would I tell? And why?

'Yeah,' Doc said, 'you're right. It's none of their damned business.'

Two months back, on the routine physical he'd been hounding me about for ages, Doc found something he didn't like. Probably nothing to it, he said, just those damn fool kids up at the lab with their e-pods. But we'd best repeat it. Then he showed up at the cabin late one night with a bottle of single malt. As usual, I'd heard his banger coming three miles down the road.

'Greeks bearing gifts—' I began.

'Are as nothing compared to an old man with a bottle of old whiskey. The old man is tired. The whiskey isn't. So we'll put it to work.'

We didn't talk much more for a while after that. Then, along about the third pour, Doc told me, just flat out and plain, like he'd mention the weather or a dog he used to have. We drank some more, and as he was leaving he started to say something, then just looked into my eyes and shook his head.

I remember how warm and quiet it was that night, and how bright the stars.

CHAPTER SIXTEEN

SOME YEARS BACK I attended a wedding, one of the guys I was in the service with, and the last contact I had, I think, with any of them. We'd been through a lot together, and his take on it was close to my own: *getting through* meant we were now somewhere else. But his wife-to-be insisted that he have one of his 'army buddies' there, so I became token grunt.

And it wasn't bad. He was marrying up, with a high-pay job awaiting him at the family firm. Even the house they'd be living in had been prepaid, so clean and white it looked as though it had been dipped in Clorox. The food was good and ample, the champagne excellent, the people, especially the women, attractive.

Barely into the ceremony, the preacher took a detour, leaving behind such commonalities as marriage vows and the couple standing there at the altar patiently waiting, to head off, instead, in praise of 'the most important union of their lives,' i.e., when they accepted Jesus Christ – a commercial announcement that went on for some time. But wind had been rising steadily, and as the preacher continued in his diversion, a powerful gust came up. It snapped the tableclothes, blew leaves sideways on the trees, and raised a twenty-foot dust devil into the air directly behind him.

A great moment.

Not that I have ever believed in portents, a belief that can only follow from the belief that there's direction at work behind the randomness of our world and lives. There are only patterns, and we make of them what we will. But sometimes, as with the preacher and the dust devil, events come together in a crazy, wonderful order.

I was thinking about that the following morning as I watched the storm build. Clouds with heavy bellies moved sluggishly about; far off I could see black pillars of rain, stabs of lightning.

Those were not the only storms building.

The guy back in the cell roused from his Van Winkle but had nothing to say, about the fake New Jersey driver's license we found on him, for instance, or about anything else except that he'd like his phone call now, thank you. He did accept a cup of coffee as he made the call, his end of the conversation consisting of *Mr Herman, please,* the name of the town, and the word *sheriff.*

Within the hour Marty was in my office.

Before retiring here, Martin Baumann had been a big-city lawyer in Chicago, corporate accounts, three-hour lunches, the works. To this day he only smiled when asked how or why, of all places, he picked this town, but once here, he soon discovered how desperately unsuited he was for leisure time and started taking the odd case. He and Val had worked together on more than one occasion, going from colleagues to friends in short order.

Marty just kind of *appeared* in the office, without fanfare, in that way he has. As though he'd been there for hours and was just now speaking up. 'You have a guest, I understand, here at the B and B. Who has, of course, been advised of his rights, blah, blah.'

Marty poured a coffee for himself and settled into Don's chair. Don was out on patrol. I'd been expecting to head to the cabin once he got back but now wondered if I might want to wait out the storm.

'What'd he do, anyway?'

I filled Marty in, and he shook his head. Took a slug or two of coffee. 'Suckers wired money, you believe that? Right into my account, damn near by the time we got off the phone.'

'Whatever's going on, these people do seem to be used to getting their way.'

'Don't seem to be much up on how things work in small towns though, do they?'

'Neither were you, as I recall.'

He shrugged. 'Fast learner. What do we know about your sleepover?'

'That he's connected to someone who can wire money—'

'A lot of money.'

'—fast.'

'That's it? Okay. Guy I spoke to was an attorney—'

'Honor among thieves?'

'An associate out of Crafft and Bailey, in St Louis. Basically a messenger boy, but with a hardball firm.'

'Not to mention confidentiality.'

'What confidentiality? I haven't even spoken with my client. How could confidentiality possibly apply?'

'Point taken.'

'I'll ask, if I need it back.' Marty did a quick rim shot on the desk edge. 'I went looking. Amazing what you can find out these days with a sidelong glance. Crafft & Bailey takes up a full two floors in a downtown high-rise, one of those places full of hardwood panels and polished mahogany rails that serve no purpose. You go in, and there'll be this huge room full of desks and cabinetry and down at the far end of it, on the horizon, a single human being.'

'You've been there.'

'More times than I care to think about. Cities are full of them. Places you could put up four or five extended families and most of the city's homeless. Empty – except, of course, for the fine appointments.'

Unsure whether or not that was a pun, I remained silent.

'Good old C&B's what the boys in the club like to call a full-service firm. One thumb in the insurance pie, defending corporations, another in plaintiff's litigation, raking it in on contingency fees. List of clients as long as the building is tall. That's the public face, and one wing of the thing. The other wing has maybe five, six clients.'

'One of them being Mr Herman.'

He tilted his head in question.

'That's the name our . . . guest, as you call him . . . brought up when he made his call.'

'Of course.' Marty refilled his cup, tasted, then poured the coffee out and set to making a fresh pot. 'Not one of them – all of them. In some guise or another. And not Herman, but Harmon. Larry, born Lorenzo, Harmon. Owns huge portions of St Louis, Chicago, and points between.'

'We talking Monopoly?'

'We're talking numbers, off-book gambling, unsecured loans, escort services, strong-arm security. Anything on the borderline between legal and otherwise, he runs it. Or his crew does. Man himself doesn't go near the action. Golfs, drinks coffee, visits his mother every morning. Two children, son about thirty, owns a ring of low-end apartments, furniture-rental stores, and the like – a very *big* ring. Named Harm, if you can believe it. Hard to say if the man's got a weird sense of humor or if he's just plain stupid oblivious. Daughter's – get this – Harmony. Word is she's so ugly everyone calls her Hominy.'

'That's who the man in my cell tracks back to.'

'Looks like.'

'And you got all this off the Internet.'

'Well, I may have made a call or two.'

'We're a long way from St Louis or Chicago. What's the connection?'

Marty poured fresh coffee for us both, set mine down on the desk. 'Why don't I go talk to my client and find out?'

CHAPTER SEVENTEEN

ETHICS BE DAMNED, as Doc would say. As he did say, in fact, when he arrived that morning to check on our guest. I had a presumed kidnapping, a presumed murder, a presumed assault or two. Doc: 'What you have is a mess.' Nothing presumptive about that.

The man's name was Troy Geldin and he hailed from Brooklyn, the old Italian section right across the river from Manhattan, now well in thrall to gentrification but resisting. State called about the time Marty emerged, an hour or so before Doc showed. They'd run prints for us. No sheet, which meant Geldin was smart, lucky, or both, but he'd done time eating sand in the elder Bush's war and we had his prints as mementos.

To this day I've no idea what Marty said to the man. I was little more than halfway into the initial sentence of my spiel when Geldin spoke over me. 'My lawyer has advised me to cooperate. After due thought and with promise of immunity, I am prepared to do so.'

Prepositional phrases and 'I am prepared' didn't sound much like Geldin's native language, but then, neither did much of what followed. At first I assumed that he'd been coached, by Marty, or by his contact during the phone call when he'd said so little. Later I came to think that, whatever the reason, something vital had shifted inside him. He had changed elementally, and something that he himself may not have suspected was there, something deep within, had begun moving to the surface. I'd seen it happen before, both in the jungle and in prison. A prickly, nervous man turns suddenly calm. The one who was always talking sits silent, smiling.

Thus it fell to me to wake Judge Ray Pitoski out of a sound sleep (albeit now almost noon), assure myself that he was sober enough to remember, and have him, as our factotum district attorney, agree to grant Geldin immunity in exchange for testimony.

That testimony came measured out in drams, like a seaman's ration. Every few sentences Geldin would pause and look from Marty to me, whether to gauge the value and effect of his testimony or to allow his next phrases to settle into place before he spoke, I couldn't tell.

Irregardless of what we thought, he was not, well, not . . . what we thought. In fact, he'd never done anything like this before. Sure, he'd lost his job a while back, after twelve years – but so had a lot of others, these days. And when his wife left, well, unlike the other, he'd seen that coming.

Hollis and he went way back, to grade school. He'd been the geeky kid back then, good grades, scrawny, out of step, always reading. Hollis was anything but, but he'd stepped in one day when the top bully, guy looked like a pug dog, had been beating on him. Not because Hollis had any feelings for him, mind you, or any sense of its being wrong, but because Hollis'd had his eye on this bully, figuring he was the one to take down. And here was his chance. Teachers came, it looked like Hollis was a hero, taking up for him. Not finessed – but sometimes finesse just happens, you know?

Anyway, that changed things for him. Year later, he was linebacker on the team. Still not fitting in, but he was good enough that they moved over to make room for him. Meanwhile Hollis went on getting into trouble, tiptoeing around this huge crater, shouting down into it. He was getting bigger, Hollis was shrinking. Took to cigarettes, got behind some serious drinking. Didn't see much of each other for a long time then, but he heard things from time to time: Hollis was boosting cars, was on the run, was doing time.

Not long after he lost his job, they met up again, neighborhood bar on Atlantic that he liked because they had no music or TV and, late morning, early afternoon, there'd be a lot of women coming through, usually in groups. They didn't recognize each other at first. Guy on the next stool looked up like him to watch three young women in gym clothes enter and said, 'Lesbo bar is what I'm thinking.' They took a closer look at each other then and realized.

Wasn't much catching up done, not a lot of talking either, after the first hour or two, but it was good to have a friend, someone to sit with, drink a few beers, someone with free time like him. And yeah, he had been wondering what Hollis did to get by, what gave him all that free time, but it's not the kind of thing you ask, once the first hints get ignored, right?

They got pretty tight over the next month or six weeks.

One afternoon, almost night really, they'd had five, six beers by then, he guessed, and the after-work crowd had started drifting in, Hollis's phone went off. He laughed at all of them reaching for their phones, then realized it was his and skipped outside to answer. Came back in time to buy the next round, and along about the third sip maybe, Hollis asked if by any chance he might be free the next couple days and up to picking up a nice chunk of change. Naturally he asked for doing what. His man had just canceled on him, Hollis said. He had a pickup to make, and sure could use the company. Nothing to it. And it paid three hundred clear.

So he said yes and found himself in this godforsaken place, no offense intended.

Things started going wrong from the first. Their flight was delayed, the woman across the aisle puked in her plastic tray of beef tips, some kid kept kicking the back of his seat. The first rental car stalled out two miles from the airport in Memphis. They had to call, wait over an hour, then take whatever was available, which turned out to be this clunky van that pulled hard to the right.

He didn't know what Hollis's intentions were, he was looking for someone, he knew that – then for something he couldn't find. By the time they got to the first house, where the old lady was, he was getting crazy, tearing up everything, hitting her – just once, but it didn't take much. It was like you could see that kid on the playground coming out of him all over again, you know? And it kept on getting worse. At the second place, he watched the woman while Hollis went through the house getting angrier all the time. It was when he realized Hollis planned on taking the woman that he got ... not scared, but ... sick. Physically ill. Heart pounding, skin crawling. Like he was going out of his body, leaving it behind.

He was in the backseat and he kept asking Hollis

to stop this, take her back, this was just flat-out crazy, and Hollis kept telling him to shut up. At one point, scooting forward in the seat, he kicked the woman's purse, which was on the floor by him. Something heavy in there. He took it out, told Hollis to stop the car, and when Hollis laughed, he shot him.

He figured there had to be a farmhouse or something somewhere, he'd carry him there and get help if he was still alive, but there wasn't. And he couldn't. He was going to call, get help for the woman too, but when Hollis died, he just got scared, really scared.

Hollis had made him memorize that phone number and name, in case anything happened to him. To Hollis, that is. He was just supposed to call, say where they were, nothing more.

And that was it. He stopped talking and sat looking down at the table, lost in thoughts of Brooklyn and the past, maybe thinking how far away that past seemed now, or maybe just used up, empty. I stopped the tape. The light outside was muted, tentative. I could hear wind coming down Main Street, the shake of roofs, the shudder of doors and windows. I smelled dust, and rain. And I felt all about me the sadness of endings.

CHAPTER EIGHTEEN

MUCH OF THE REST of the story, we got from Milly two days later up in Memphis, what she'd pieced together from Troy's and Hollis's jagged conversation. She was propped up in bed, leg in traction, tubes running out of her chest into a Pleurovac, right arm in a cast. One or another caretaker, a nurse, an aide, had brushed her hair on the right, the left side having been shaved and stitched, and (at Milly's request?) put on blush and lipstick, unsettling against the bruises and wormy scars. She looked half little girl's doll, half ghoul.

It was all about something Billy'd got messed up in. Something he'd stolen, or found, or was holding, she still didn't know. Didn't know where either, if it was here before he left, or up in Hazelwood, but she thought Hazelwood.

The driver kept saying he had a job to do and his ass was dirt if he didn't get it done and these hicks were getting seriously in his way and on his nerves. First time he said that, she thought he said 'ticks.' The other one kept patting her on the shoulder, telling her it was going to be all right, and asking the driver, What are you going to do with the woman, Hollis, she can't help you. Telling him to pull over, stop. She remembered the driver laughing and not much after that.

Someone had been in the house, she was sure of that when she got home. Just didn't *feel* right. She never drank Cokes, and if she did she would never leave a can on the sink but there was one there, that had probably been in the icebox since Billy left. He was the Coke drinker. Then she noticed a few other things. Kitchen drawers weren't pushed shut, the door to the basement had been opened – you could tell because it was right next to the water heater and the paint kind of half-melted so the door stuck in the frame, then tore loose when it was opened. Things like that. She didn't know why, she hadn't even thought about the gun, all but forgot it was there, but before she knew it she'd gone in the bedroom and got it, shoved it in her purse. Then she kept the purse with her as she went through the house turning on lights. They were standing outside, behind the house, when she snapped on the lights back there. And she just stood there as they came in.

'One of them's dead,' she said. 'A nurse told me that.' Her eyes were fixed not on mine but on the wall over my shoulder. When I took a step closer, she looked away.

'And we have the other one.'

She reached up to readjust the NG tube, nostril reddened and crusty around it. 'He tried to help me.'

'Yes.'

'His friend's dead.'

I nodded.

'I was almost dead,' she said.

'You're going to be okay.'

'And Billy's dead.'

'Yes. Yes, he is.'

Before leaving we spoke with Milly's doctor, a thin, gangly woman of indeterminate nationality wearing a black T-shirt, scrub pants, and cheap white sneakers without socks. Physically, she said, there was every expectation that Milly would make a full recovery. She was showing signs of traumatic amnesia, remembering things then forgetting them, but with luck, and obviously she was due some, that should pass as well. It's similar to a short circuit, Dr Paul said. The spark gets sent, there's power in the wires, sometimes the bulb lights, sometimes it doesn't. Or it flickers and goes out.

Lonnie was silent most of the way back to town, looking out the side window. Many fields remained partially under water; trees and the occasional power or telephone line were down. Here and there, blackbirds and crows crowded together at water's edge, covens of diminutive priests.

'You look back much, Turner? How things were?'

'Sure I do.'

'Lot back there.'

'At least, if we're lucky, it's not gaining on us.'

'But it rears up and grabs us sooner or later, doesn't it?'

Does it? Patterns. You make of them what you will.

'She's going to be okay, Lonnie. She'll get over it.'

'Of course. And so will Shirley, from our losing Billy. That's what we do.' He turned from the window to look straight ahead. 'I'm just damn tired of getting over things, Turner.'

To our right, westward, over past Kansas and Oklahoma, the sun was sinking. As delta, cropland, and congregations of crows rolled by beside us, I told Lonnie what Doc had told me that night at the cabin, and when I was through he didn't say anything about miracles or prayers or remission, as I knew he wouldn't, he just sat there a moment, looked over at me and said, 'That sucks too.'

CHAPTER NINETEEN

'NOT THE BEST DECISION you ever made;' I told Lonnie three days later. We were back in Memphis, waiting at the airport. Lonnie was flying to St Louis and I'd driven him up. At check-in he'd flashed his badge to account for the handgun in his luggage. That was another argument I'd lost, just as I – not to mention Shirley, Doc and Don Lee – had lost the one about his going in the first place.

'Could be one of the worst,' he said. 'But I want to look at him face-to-face and tell him what he's done.'

'He knows what he's done, Lonnie. He doesn't care. And he's not the kind of man it's easy to get face-to-face with.'

'I'll manage.'

Doubtless he would. There was no one for whom

I had more respect than I had for Lonnie Bates, no one I thought smarter or more capable. I didn't know what he was feeling about Billy's death. We can never know how others feel, however much we pretend. I hoped it wasn't guilt. Guilt is a treacherous motivator.

Should you ever want a cross-section of America's minions, airports like this are where you'll find it. Students in torn jeans and T-shirts or in goth black and rattling when they walk; businessmen with one ear flattened from chronic cell phone use; families with groaning luggage carts topped by a stuffed bear; shell-shocked travelers who keep pulling tickets and itineraries out of pockets or purses and going back up to the check-in desk to ask questions; solitary men and women who sit staring ahead hardly moving until their flight is called; fidgeters and tap dancers and sub voce singers whose tonsils you see jumping in their cage; faces lit by faint hope that where they are going will be a happier, a better, a more tolerant, or at least a less painful place than the one they're leaving.

I remembered part of a poem Cy put in a letter: *The way your life is ruined here, in this small corner of the world, is the way it's ruined everywhere.* I had that quote on my cell wall for months. Strange, what can give you solace.

Lonnie was drinking coffee out of a plastic cup large enough to be used as a bucket to extinguish small fires. It had boxes to be checked on the side, showing all the choices available to us out here in the free world, and, at the top, vents vaguely reminiscent of gills.

Besides the quote, I was also remembering Cy's story about a client of his, one of those he called cyclers, people who come for a while, fade out, return. Guy'd been away most of a year and was so changed that Cy barely recognized him. Like looking at a mask, trying to make out the features beneath, Cy said. In the course of conversation Cy asked where he was living these days. The man looked around, as though he were trying the room on for size (again, Cy's analogy), and said 'Mostly in the past.' He was at work, he explained, on a major project, The Museum of Real America. What he was doing was collecting signs people held up at the side of the road. He'd give them a dollar or two. STRANDED. WILL WORK FOR FOOD. HOMELESS GOD BLESS. VETERAN – TWICE. Had over thirty of them now. Quite a display.

Lonnie spoke beside me. 'I can remember rushing through the airport at the last minute, jumping on the plane just as they pulled up the gangway. Now you have to arrive two hours ahead, bring a note from your mother, walk through hoops, have dogs sniff you. Take off your goddamn shoes.'

'Anyone tell you you're beginning to sound like Doc?'

His eyes moved to watch parents greet a young man coming down the corridor from the plane he'd be taking, then shifted back. 'Things just get harder and harder, Turner.'

He was right, of course. Things get harder, and we get soft. Or, some of us, we harden too, less and less of the world making it through to us.

'June tell you she was getting married?'

She hadn't.

'Her so-called gardener,' Lonnie went on. 'Man mows yards for a living, is what he does. This August. She wanted to ask you ... But I guess I'd best leave that between the two of you.'

Lonnie hadn't said anything more after our conversation in the Jeep coming home from Memphis three days back, but the awareness was there in his eyes, and for that moment I could feel it moving about in the narrow space between us. The world is so very full of words. And yet so much that's important goes forever unsaid.

Minutes later Lonnie's flight was called. I stood watching his plane taxi out, wait its turn, and begin its plunge, thinking about power, gravity's pride, about that magic moment when the ground lets go and you're weightless, free.

I had no idea what awaited my friend.

On the drive back, I rummaged in the glove compartment and found the tape I'd made of Eldon and Val playing together years back on a slow Sunday afternoon of potato salad, grilled chicken and burgers, beer and iced tea. At first the tape spun without purchase and I was afraid it had broken or snagged, then Val's banjo came in, Eldon's guitar sifting quiet chords and bass runs behind her as she began singing.

> The engine whistled down the line
> A-blowing every station: McKinley's dying
> From Buffalo to Washington

The sky was eerily clear and bright as I coursed along listening to the two of them. After all I've seen in this life, I'm not an emotional man, but I could feel tears building, trying to push through. Two good friends gone.

I'd done my best to dissuade Lonnie right up to the end. Finally, knowing that was not going to happen, having known it from the first but dead set on trying, I handed him the package. We had just taken seats in the terminal. A line of German tourists wearing identical sweaters debarked from a plane painted with snowcaps, icy streams, and blue-white skies, as though it were its own small, mobile country.

'What the hell is this?'

'A sled, as far as I can tell.'

Ignoring or innocent of my reference, he waited.

'I started thinking, and went back to the car, the Buick that Billy was driving. I called and found out it was still in Hazelwood while the city tried to figure out what to do with it, so I took Sonny and went up there. Anyone knows cars, it's Sonny. Sergeant Haskell arranged for us to use the garage that does all the work for the police department and city. Sonny kept asking me, What are you looking for? Hell if I knew.

'He started tearing the Buick down, poking around. Before long, the mechanic who owns the garage came over and started talking shop with Sonny. Next thing I know he's under the car working away too.

'After a while, Sonny finds me outside. "Well, we know what caused it," he tells me. The wreck, he means, why Billy plowed into City Hall. Looks like a tie rod disconnect, he said. Car'd been sitting up unused, then gets driven hard – not that surprising.

'He goes back inside. Maybe a half hour, a little more, passes. Then he brings out this package, wrapped in what looks like canvas or oilcloth – turned out to be an old chamois – with twine around it in a crisscross. The knot on the twine is a perfect bow. Inside the chamois there's a box with a faded silk scarf, another crisscross, this one of ribbon, and a tiny ball, like a Christmas-tree ornament. Thing had been under the seat, jammed into the springs.

'It's a necklace,' I told Lonnie. 'Silver, underneath a few decades of tarnish. Engraved inside with two small hearts, one with the initials LH, the other with AC.'

'LH . . .'

'Could well be Lorenzo Harmon. AC is Augusta Chorley.'

'The old lady.'

'She wasn't always old, Lonnie. And it appears that her life may not have been as empty as everyone thought. She really did have a treasure out there, albeit it a personal one.'

He held the package up, weighing it, thinking, I'm sure, of the damage that had accured around it. 'And Billy?'

'A messenger, maybe, delivering the necklace to someone here in town, or up in Memphis – with or without Miss Chorley's knowledge. Or it could only be that the necklace has been in the car all these years, forgotten.'

'Here we've been thinking this whole thing had to do with money, drugs—'

'The usual suspects, yes. And it still may have. The necklace could be coincidence.'

'That's a lot of maybes.'

I spread my hands in mock resignation. 'Go have your face-to-face with Harmon. If you choose to, give the necklace to him. For good or bad – I've no idea. See what happens.'

'I'd be finishing Billy's job.'

Again I spread my hands at the world's uncertainties, its unreadability.

As afterwards, driving home alone in the Jeep, listening to Eldon and Val, I shrugged at the same. Briefly Val returned to one of the old mountain tunings, sawmill or double C, then came the hard stutter of clawhammer, and her voice.

> Li'l birdie, li'l birdie
> Come sing to me a song
> I've a short while to be here
> And a long time to be gone

CHAPTER TWENTY

SO MANY STORIES LEAVE YOU standing at the altar. The crisis has been met, the many obstacles averted or overcome, most everything's back to the way it was before or has righted itself to some new still point. You always wonder what happened to these people. Because they had pasts, they had lives, before you began reading. And they have futures, some of them, once you stop.

I remember a story I read years ago, hanging at a newsstand on Lamar waiting for the bar across the street to open for the day. Must have been the early seventies. I wasn't long out of Nam. On the first page this young guy stands on a hill looking down into the valley where the worms that tried to take over the world are dead and dying. He did that. He saved the world. Then for the next ten pages and the rest of his life he's living in a trailer park drinking beer for breakfast and bouncing off bad relationships.

That's pretty much how it goes, for most of us. We don't stub our toes on streets of gold and lead rich lives, we don't tell the people we love how much we love them when it matters, we never quite inhabit the shadows we cast as we cross this world. We just go on.

And some of us, a self-chosen few, go about finding how much music we can make with what we have left.

In my dream that night I couldn't find the town I live in. Friends and family awaited me, I knew, and I had started out for home hours before but somehow kept losing my way. Parts of the town, certain streets and buildings, looked familiar, others didn't, and I was always close, always *almost* home, but could never make it there. Occasionally in the distance I would catch glimpses of the sea, of high-rise buildings, of missile silos and grain elevators, of clouds and darkening sky.

I didn't go home or to the office that day upon returning from Memphis. Instead I did something I'd been putting off a long time.

The house had sat empty since the day Val died. I kept telling myself I should go over there, and thinking about it, but there was always a swing through the town in the Jeep that needed doing, or paperwork to attend to, or one more cup of coffee to drink at the diner, and I never did.

It didn't look greatly different from the outside, simply abandoned. I thought of faces – I'd seen a lot of them, in prison, and in my practice – that showed no emotion. Weather had had its way with roof and windows, and a tree nearby had split down the length of its trunk, taking out half a room at the back. Runners had advanced (the word *politely* came to mind) onto porch and sides.

I don't know what I expected to find, save memories. But I certainly didn't expect to find what I did. I used the key Val had given me when she planned to go on the road with Eldon, stepped in, and stopped just inside the door. As handy with a hammer or saw as with a banjo (her words), Val had been at work restoring the old house since before we met. Three rooms had been pretty much done, as far as basics go – framework, floors, walls.

Now it was all but finished.

I went from room to room: smooth hardwood banisters, coving expertly fitted at juncture of floor and wall, inlays of tile at thresholds, crown molding curved like bird wings overhead, two-tone paint in most rooms, what looked like period wallpaper in a couple of them. It was stunning.

Someone had spent a lot of time in here. Someone

with amazing skill. And with motivations I couldn't even begin to guess at.

In this small town where we all know one another's business, or think we do. 'Round here you sneeze, Doc says, and the people four houses down yell Bless you.

Ever the lawyer, Val, as we found out following her death, had a will on file. The house was mine. I stood wondering, trying to imagine who might be moved to come here day after day, month after month, to do all this work, and what that person's reasons could possibly be.

Maybe, like so much in life, reason had little to do with it.

Then puzzlement turned to laughter at the sheer, wonderful craziness of this. You get to be my age, you figure life doesn't have many surprises left for you. And here I was, in my dead girlfriend's house that time and weather had done its best to destroy and that someone had gone hell-bent on bringing back to life.

I sat there most of the afternoon, on the floor, out on the porch, out under one of the trees, marveling.

CHAPTER TWENTY-ONE

BACK TO STORIES, then. Here's where we are. Here's what happened.

Next day, a little after noon but decidedly dark for that hour, I'm sitting outside the office in an all-but-deserted downtown. Lonnie is in St Louis doing what he feels he has to do. Milly lies slowly fitting the pieces of her world back together in a Memphis hospital room. Val's house, my house, having withstood well over a hundred years of ravage and neglect, stands waiting for the blows that finally will bring it down. The weather service has announced a major storm heading directly toward us, torrential rains, sixty-mile-an-hour winds, funnel clouds. We can see it already in this plum-dark sky, smell it on the breeze beginning to assert itself, as lights go on in houses at town's edge. Birds have taken to, then deserted, the wires. Dogs bay in the distance.

The storm is coming in. And the town, in its last hour, is waiting.

My daughter sits beside me.

An hour ago the door opened, right beside the new window we at last got installed, and there she was. Longer hair, but looking much the same. Except for fresh stitches over one eye.

'Nice scar.'

'Important thing is, he came around to my way of thinking.'

'I'll bet he did.'

After a moment she said, 'Doc Oldham called.'

'Man's a public nuisance.'

We made coffee and sat around catching up, like so many times before. As though nothing were different. Her department had put in a computer system no one could figure out, there was a new drug on the street, last month they'd had a murder in, of all places, the Wal-Mart parking lot. I filled her in on Billy, Eldon, and the rest. Told her about Val's house. And how not long before she arrived, Isaiah Stillman and a group from the colony had come walking down Main Street, saying they were here to do what they could to help.

At her suggestion we took the last of the coffee outside and sat on the bench polished by a generation or so of butts.

'Good seat for the show,' she said.

'Best in the house.'

So here we are. The air is charged, electric. I think back to Lonnie's plane, that moment just before the ground lets go. That's what it feels like.

Takeoffs. Landings. And the lives that happen in between.

'Thought I might stick around a while, if that's all right,' J. T. says.

'Probably ought to be my line.' We both laugh. 'Though from the look of things . . .'

'Who knows. Could be I'll spot my first airborne cow.'

'There you go, Miss City Dweller. Having your fun at the poor rural folks' expense.'

Cabbages and kings don't come into it, as I recall, but, sitting there on the bench, we touch on close to everything else: J. T.'s childhood, my old partner on the MPD and my prison time, genealogy, where the country is headed politically, a novel she'd recently read about small-town life, the day Kennedy died, beer for breakfast back in Nam, third-strike offenders, Val.

Then we sit quietly, for an hour, maybe more, as black thunderheads roll in. Initially we see the jags of lightning and hear the muffled rumbling only through the dark screen of clouds. Then it breaks through. The rain, when it comes, is sweet and stinging.

A heavy metal trash can rolls down the street, driven

by wind. 'City tumbleweed,' J. T. says, and when I look at her there are tears in her eyes. I reach and touch her face, gently.

'I'm not crying because I'm sad,' my daughter says. 'I'm crying because we're here, together, watching this, I'm crying because of friends like Doc Oldham, because I have had the chance to get to know you. I am crying because the world is so beautiful.'

As should we all.

A NOTE ON THE AUTHOR

James Sallis is the author of more than two dozen volumes of fiction, poetry, translation, essays, and criticism, including the Lew Griffin cycle, *Drive, Cypress Grove*, and *Cripple Creek*. His biography of the great crime writer Chester Himes is an acknowledged classic. Sallis lives in Phoenix, Arizona, with his wife, Karyn, and an enormous white cat.

DRIVE
by James Sallis

'I drive. That's what I do. All I do.'

'Much later, as he sat with his back against an inside wall of a Motel 6 just north of Phoenix, watching the pool of blood lap toward him, Driver would wonder whether he had made a terrible mistake. Later still, of course, there'd be no doubt. But for now Driver is, as they say, in the moment. And the moment includes this blood lapping toward him, the pressure of dawn's late light at windows and door, traffic sounds from the interstate nearby, the sound of someone weeping in the next room . . .'

Thus begins *Drive,* a novella by James Sallis. Set mostly in Arizona and L.A., the story is, according to Sallis, '. . . about a guy who does stunt driving for movies by day and drives for criminals at night. In classic noir fashion, he is double-crossed and, though before he has never participated in the violence ('I drive. That's all.'), he goes after the ones who double-crossed and tried to kill him.'

'Sallis creates vivid images in very few words and his taut, pared-down prose is distinctive and powerful. The result is a small masterpiece.' – *The Sunday Telegraph*

CYPRESS GROVE
by James Sallis

The small town where Turner moved is one of America's lost places, halfway between Memphis and forever. That makes it a perfect hide-away; a place where you can bury the past and escape the pain of human contact, where you are left alone unless you want company, where conversation happens only when there's something to say, where you can sit and watch an owl fly silently across the face of the moon. And where Turner hoped to forget that he was a cop, a psychotherapist, and always an ex-con.

There was no major crime to speak of until Sheriff Lonnie Bates arrived on Turner's porch with a bottle of Wild Turkey and a problem; the body of a drifter has been found – brutally and ritualistically murdered – and Bates and his deputy need help from someone with big-city experience who appreciates the delicacy of investigating people in a small town. Thrust back into the middle of what he left behind, Turner slowly becomes reacquainted not only with the darkness he had fled, but with the unsuspected kindness of others.

'James Sallis is a superb writer' – *The Times*

Please send orders to:
Oldcastle Books (SR08), 21 Great Ormond Street,
London, WC1N 3JB

Add 15% P&P. Cheque's payable to Oldcastle Books in Sterling drawn on UK bank or pay by credit card (Visa, MC, Maestro) quoting card number, expiry date, 3 digit security code, and Valid from date and Issue number where appropriate

Tel: 020 7430 1021   Fax: 020 7430 0021
Order online at www.noexit.co.uk

CRIPPLE CREEK
by James Sallis

A year or so has passed since the events of *Cypress Grove*. Ex-policeman, ex-con, former therapist, Turner has become Deputy Sheriff in the small town within driving distance of Memphis, Tennessee, to which he had migrated in hopes of escaping his past. His life is mending as he and Val Bjorn grow closer. And then a young man, arrested on a routine traffic stop with more than $200,000 in his trunk, is forcibly sprung from jail after Sheriff Don Lee is brutally assaulted. Throwing caution aside, Turner goes in pursuit to Memphis, unleashing ghosts he thought he had left behind, and endangering all that matters to him now.

'Sallis is an unsung genius of crime writing. Hunt this one out and you won't be disappointed.' – *The Independent*

Please send orders to:
Oldcastle Books (SR08), 21 Great Ormond Street,
London, WC1N 3JB

Add 15% P&P. Cheque's payable to Oldcastle Books in Sterling drawn on UK bank or pay by credit card (Visa, MC, Maestro) quoting card number, expiry date, 3 digit security code, and Valid from date and Issue number where appropriate

Tel: 020 7430 1021   Fax: 020 7430 0021
Order online at www.noexit.co.uk